Bask

BASK

UNSINKABLE

How to Be Alive, Rich, and Free

SID HUSTON
Editor Terrie Solheim

Printed in the United States

Paperback ISBN: 979-8-9947484-0-4
Ebook ISBN: 979-8-9947484-1-1

Contents

Other Books by
Sid Huston

From the *BASK Series of Christian Fiction*

BASK: Real Spirituality

BASK: Wisdom

BASK: Sexual Freedom and Sexual Restraint

BASK: Satisfaction

BASK: Barnacles

BASK: Sunshine

BASK: Pirate Greed

Pirate Speak

Insights that will help you break the pirate code!

Addled: *To be mad or insane, maybe just plain stupid*

Ahoy: *Hello*

Avast: *Hold fast, stop and pay attention*

Aye: *A pirate way of saying yes, but ye never really know if he means it*

Begad: *By God!*

Bilge: *The lowest part of the ship inside the hull along the keel; thus, nonsense or foolish talk—how low can you go?*

Bilge-sucking: *Uncomplimentary expression*

Blaggard: *An insult or a scoundrel*

Blouse: *A loose-fitting shirt*

Booty: *Loot*

Boucan Knife: *A quick-strike weapon used to hack and slash to overpower others, kept hidden under the blouse*

Buccaneer: *Caribbean pirates*

Bucko: *Used as "me bucko," "my friend"*

Bunghole: *Food was stored in wooden casks, and the stopper in the barrel was called the bung. Pirate food was bad, so being called a bunghole wasn't a compliment.*

C or Sí: *A Spanish pirate term for "yes!"*

Cap'n: *Short for Captain*

Cat-o'-nine-tails: *Or cat, for a whip made of nine leather straps used for flogging; it will smarten you up!*

Chase: *Ship being pursued*

Cockswain: *The Cap'n's attendant, one who would do the rowing*

Corsair: *A romantic term for pirate*

Crow's-Nest: *The platform near the top of the mast, a position for a lookout*

Cutlass: *A curved sword*

Cutter: *A single-masted sailing vessel that is rigged fore and aft with two or more head sails.*

Dance the Hempen Jig: *To hang from a noose made of hemp*

Davy Jones's locker: *The bottom of the sea*

Dead Men Tell No Tales: *A dead man cannot betray you with their secrets; therefore, a pirate would much rather turn them into shark bait, so that they could not bite them back by telling something incriminating.*

Doldrums: *Your ship is on the sea with no wind in your sails. A time of inactivity and stagnation, life is dull, listless, and the crew is depressed. When sailing men are in the doldrums, you just never know what stupid things they will do.*

Doubloon: *A Spanish gold coin*

Feed the Fish: *When you are thrown overboard*

Freebooter: *A pirate, one who seeks to live free by plundering others, a buccaneer*

Gangplank: *A removable footway between the ship and the pier, also known as the gangway*

Gangway: *"Get out of my way."*

Go on Account: *To become a pirate*

Godspeed: *Good-bye and good luck*

Grog: *An alcoholic drink; pirates prefer rum*

Hornswaggle: *To cheat or defraud; to act like a pirate*

I or Aye: *"Yes"*

Jolly Roger: *The pirates' skull and crossbones flag, an invitation to surrender*

Kiss the Gunner's Daughter: *Punishment; to be bent over a cannon and flogged*

Lad, Lass, Lassie: *Someone younger than you, e.g., a boy or youth, a girl, or young woman (lass and lassie are females)*

Land Ho: *A sailor's cry to announce the sight of land and a way to say "watch out, rum, here I come."*

Landlubber: *"Lubber," an old English term for being big, slow, clumsy, not very skilled, as if they said, "I bet you were no better on land."*

Letters of Marque: *Papers used by a national government, entitling a private seagoing vessel to raid enemy commerce*

Maroon: *To be abandoned and deserted; a convenient way for pirates to get rid of someone without actually killing him*

Matey: *A cheerful and friendly pirate address*

Me Hearties: *A way a Cap'n would address his crew*

Picaroon: *A Spanish term of derision meaning a rascal*

Piece of Eight: *A Spanish silver coin that could be cut into eight pieces*

Pillage: *To raid, rob, and sack*

Pirate: *A seagoing robber and murderer*

Port: *A seaport*

Privateer: *An armed private ship authorized by a country's government with Letters of Marque to attack foreign ships. Often their goal was to capture foreign ships rather than sink them. They were paid to raid, and then they would divide the loot with their sponsoring government, the investors, and the crew.*

R or Arrrr: *Glee*

Rum: *A traditional pirate alcoholic drink*

Sail Ho!: *"I see a ship."*

Scuppers: *Spaces on the deck edge which allow water to drain back into the sea*

Scurvy: *A disease caused by the lack of vitamin C; a bad sickness, and a derogatory term, "ye scurvy dogs"*

Sea Dog: *A very experienced sailor, one with lots of stories to tell, stories that always get bigger and better with time*

Shark Bait: *Your foes are about to feed the fish, or a worthless and lazy sailor, a "lubber."*

Shiver Me Timbers: *Shock or disbelief, perhaps from the shock of running the ship into a reef or from being hit with a cannon ball*

Shipshape: *A well-organized ship, under control, finished, or complete*

Sink Me: *Surprise*

Splicing the Main Brace: *After a strong storm or a fierce sea battle, when the main brace that held the main sail was broken, it would have to be repaired. It would have to be spliced together with another pole. This was dangerous work. Ropes would have to be held steady, and hemp rope would be used to wrap or splice the brace. The man in charge would reward this effort by giving his sailors an extra ration of rum. Today this phrase is a euphemism for "let's go get drunk."*

Swashbuckling: *Having the exciting manner or behavior of pirates, especially those depicted in films (obsolete,* ***swash*** *to make the noise of a sword striking a shield +* ***buckler*** *[shield])*

Walking the Plank: *A severe form of punishment where someone would be forced to walk a long and narrow piece of wood (a plank) off the boat and end up making a splash in the cold wet water. AKA "shark bait."*

Yo-ho-ho: *A pirate thing to say*

Port Royal, a Place of Pleasure

Once upon a time, prior to June 7, 1692, there was a place of pleasure called Port Royal. It was a beautiful natural harbor with waters deep enough for the large ships during this "Golden Age of Piracy." It was an unusual place, as if pirates had hung a "Pirates Welcome Here" sign at the mouth of the bay.

The early history of Jamaica has the indigenous peoples called the Arawaks, also known as the Tainos, sailing from northern South America in dugout canoes. These canoes were incredible handmade marvels, as they could accommodate as many as 80 people. They were made from the trunk of a tree and carved by hand. These were mild people who were farmers and fishers who enjoyed a good smoke. They grew tobacco, maize, cassis, potatoes, sweet potatoes, beans, peanuts, peppers, pumpkin, guava, pineapple and gourds. This indeed was an island paradise filled with pleasures. They called this island Xaymaca, "a land of wood and water."

Later, French explorers would visit the island, and it remained a very pleasant place. Then in 1494, Christopher Columbus flexed Spanish muscle and brought his sharp-edged steel sword. He mocked the natives because they were so amiable and only had sticks for fighting. Columbus had been lied to by the Cubans; he was told that there was gold in Jamaica. Because there is no gold in Jamaica, he was very disappointed and showed his displeasure to these natives. He provoked fights, and in little time and with little effort, he planted the Spanish flag on the island, claiming it for Spain.

In the 1650s, this island was tugged away from the Spanish by the English in two decisive battles in 1657 and 1658. Governor Edward D'Oyley came up with a novel idea: to make the much-desired Port Royal Bay into a pirate haven. A place for pirates, managed and defended by pirates.

He hand-picked the famous swashbuckler (Sir) Captain Henry Morgan for the job. He had a proud and rich record of defrauding the Spanish coastal cities and ships of their gold, silver, and jewels. He had the respect of pirates everywhere because he was a legend on the seas and a wealthy sea robber, feared for his ruthless reputation, and esteemed because of his power and authority.

He compiled laws and rules for the "Brethren of the Coast." Originally Protestant refugees from France and Great Britain who settled in Hispaniola, they were a loose syndicate of pirates and buccaneers, exchanging supplies for guns and ammunition. After being robbed by the Spanish and driven out of Hispaniola, Governor D'Oyley invited the Brethren to make Port Royal their home port.

Henry Morgan donned a red silk suit with all the accoutrements (gold, brass buckles, boots, and blunderbuss guns) and was known for recruiting skilled sailing men because of his prowess and his reputation for outmaneuvering the Spanish at Maracaibo. He drew former servants, soldiers, sailors, and log-cutters (carpenters) to join his crew. He had made his men rich, and they coveted their success with him. When they came into Port Royal, Morgan—who was now a captain—made this place a paradise for pirates. He even developed a local currency so his crew could purchase every pleasure they coveted. It wasn't long after his ships landed before his men were "howling at the moon" like a pack of happy wolves.

Captain Morgan had the clout, capacity, and audacity to make things happen for pirates in Port Royal. He went right to work making this port a place for pleasure for his pirates. Even though He wanted to be known as a privateer (one employed by a government or business), he was a pirate at heart and had a way with pirates. He understood the appetites of his men; he accommodated their *scurvy pirate flesh* with delectable pleasures.

He knew this port was a strategic location for trade. There were lots of commodities to trade, and about one-half of the population were slaves who had landed from Africa. So, in this coveted, beautiful spot, there was forced trade, slave trade, sex-trade and the trading of goods and "services." The area was rich in sugarcane, tobacco, rum, beer, wine, grog, fruits, and vegetables, and a beautiful clime to boot. He just knew that pirates would love this cove, and he went to great lengths to make sure this was a protected port for all the businesses he wanted to traffic in. He knew the trade winds would blow riches his way.

To protect this port, he built a defense system with at least five forts at all sides of the inlet positioned to defend the area from the Spanish and others who wouldn't play by his rules. Here he had a place for careening, where ships could be laid over on their side, the cargo removed, and the barnacles scraped off the bottom of the boat. He made sure there were taverns serving grog, beer, and wine, so his fans would be able to *splice the main brace*, while the ships were being repaired. He wanted the men to "repair" while they were there. He knew this was going to be a good and profitable business.

Famous pirates made Port Royal their hangout, but it was the women who put Port Royal on the map. The hospitality of "No Conscience Nan," "Salt-Beef Peg," "Buttock-De-Clink Jenny," and Mary Carleton made sailing men around the West Indies want to visit these colorful prostitutes. Even their tag-line names went out on the trade winds as advertising and made Port Royal the go-to destination for sailing men. Captain Morgan made a deal with the authorities in London. He would repurpose the troubled girls and young women the authorities had picked up and delivered them to Port Royal, where a madam would train them in the sex trade. The whores of Port Royal were a pleasure sailing man wanted to experience. They advertised their wares on the boardwalk with gusto and the whistling and howling would follow.

Soon, the 51 acres around the bay of Port Royal were filled with 2,000 buildings. Some were four stories high, with cellars, tiled roofs, and sash windows like you would see in London. Six hundred were made of brick, and the rest were built with wood. There was a lot of bustling going on in this city. There were merchants offering fine clothing, shoes, and accessories. Tradesmen who made exquisite goods. The governor's house was located there. There were many inns and at least 70 taverns to accommodate these playful visitors. There were even four churches in the area, which is a bit weird for the place everyone knew to be the wickedest place on Earth. It was also the richest.

When a ship pulled into port, they were greeted with a gun salute. The townspeople ran to the dock to greet them. Work stopped and the people admired the prize. They all had their way of providing something to wiggle the gold, silver, pearls, and jewels out of the pockets of these visitors. There would be a price to pay for docking. The governor got a portion of one-twelfth; the admiral received a one-tenth piece of the action, and the king took one-fifth, or 20%. The British have always loved their taxes.

As the sailing men bolted off the ship, some were looking for a bath. Others wanted some fresh food. But most ran to one of the taverns for some rum, wine, grog, or beer. They just wanted to *splice the main brace* and get sloshing drunk. Most wanted the services of the whores and to experience the sensual pleasure they had been dreaming about while at sea. For certain, everyone was happy to be off a creaking-rocking ship that smelled of bilge water. Just happy not to eat hard tack, or rat dung-infested soggy tack, depending on how much bilge water made its way into the cask.

Soon they would be playing dominoes, watching cock fights, and gambling on them. They would be purchasing trinkets, shooting billiards, and sitting around the bars and taverns, telling exaggerated stories about their exploits. For all of this pleasure, the loot in their pockets would dwindle, and, in a short time, they would be begging their captain to go raiding again. But for now, they would eat well (bread, smoked beef, fruit, roasted chicken, fruits and vegetables), drink well (lemonade punch, brandy, cacao drink with molasses), and rest on a real bed made with feathers or siesta on a comfortable hammock. This was, indeed, a place of pleasure.

Chew on This: God is the God of pleasure. So, what is wrong with loving pleasure? Didn't God make all these good things? How are we to enjoy God and pleasure without sinning? "Those who love pleasure become poor" (Proverbs 21:17, NLT).

Crashing Waves

Sid Huston

(To the tune of “How Firm a Foundation”)

How daunting are the waves
The struggles of life I endure

They can tear me apart
Even my dreams can be swept away

Just when I think I stand
The riptide pulls me down

I dig in my feet
But as the water heaves, I sway

Feeling unstable like a drunk sailor
Crashing waves take me under

Fear grips my weary soul
Asking, is my life a total loss?

The surge tests my nerve
Rocked by the moving ridge

Am I going under for good?
Or will I rise again and live?

In this moment of rushing power
Will I be dour? Or will I flower?

These crashing waves bury me
Yet, I am like seed. I will sprout and see

I see the best thing is the death of me
Daily I die, because I believe

Rising above the brutal surf
I see that my life has worth

Now I want to live fully
These crashing waves have truly tested me

Resolved: I will live what I believe
God's imperishable seed has made me see

When the deep heap comes over me
I will choose to lift my head, because I believe.

"I hear the tumult of the raging seas as your
waves and surging tides sweep over
me. But each day the Lord
pours his unfailing love upon me, and
through each night, I sing his songs, praying to
God who gives me life" (Psalm 42:7–8, NLT).

The "Swashbuckler"

In the history of the world, few people have been as colorful as the swashbuckler Captain Henry Morgan. His red silk suit and handlebar moustache set him apart. His recruiting techniques and his tactics made him successful. Men would brag that they sailed with this man. Men became incredibly rich because they raided with this man. Men had a barrel of fun because they partied with this man. Men would howl at the moon because this man took care of their fantasies.

This Welshman would sail with Vice Admiral Sir Christopher Myngs. Spanish Jamaica was captured by the British in May 1655, under a plan conceived by Oliver Cromwell, known as the Western Design. In 1662, Myngs promised his men "unbridled plunder," and they attacked Santiago de Cuba. He shared the bounty with his buccaneers.

In 1663, Myngs and Edward Mansvelt had assembled a large buccaneer fleet with 1,400 men—including Henry Morgan—where they went on to sack Campeche, Mexico.

Myngs developed a reputation for unnecessary cruelty and making large hauls of silver and gold. In 1659, he raided Cumaná, Puerto Cabello, and Coro, seizing 20 chests of silver. Young Morgan was taking notes and learning lessons. He quickly learned that the loot had a way of appeasing the crew and the authorities. And the cruelty he noted meant business, serious business.

Myngs would disobey orders from Governor Edward D'Oyley of Jamaica and shared a quarter of a million pounds with his buckoes. D'Oyley had him arrested for embezzlement and returned him to England to be tried in 1660 on the *Marstan Moor.*

Morgan observed how the men were highly motivated by the lure of the loot. Therefore, he incorporated significant pay, which led to the giddiness of having money in one's pocket when he would reward his crew. *Sink me*, Morgan knew the way to a sailing man's soul, and he took a deep dive.

The Swashbuckler also learned that liquor had a way of loosening up the men. He would do some of his recruiting in the taverns, and the hooch had the men chomping on the bit for an opportunity to sail and raid with him. His image as the flamboyant sea captain was a shtick he played like a well-tuned fiddle. He also lured them with the smell of money. He was rich, and he was all about making people rich, even all of Port Royal.

The red silk suit, the boots, and the allure of the booty had the excitable recruits talking, and he knew how to get positive attention to lean his way. The more they drank, the more they talked, and he talked them right on to his ships. Before you could say *shiver me timbers*, they were signing articles of agreement and, in a way, signing their lives away. Men wanted to run with this eccentric winner. His legacy would be that of making people rich, but none richer than himself. He would abscond with the gold and silver, too, in a manner much like Myng's.

Morgan was a learner and he had lots of good ideas. He even provided his crew with insurance in the form of compensation for injured workers. Pirating was rough and dangerous. If a crewmember could lose an eye, he provided more than an eye patch. An extra portion of the booty to cover the loss of an eye. If someone lost an arm, there was a price for that, too. If a sailor lost their leg, he would help them acquire a peg and pay a price for their loss. He placed a high value on the ship's surgeon and medications, and the medical chest was a prized possession on any ship. There were painkillers and remedies for several afflictions.

The swashbuckler had a legacy of success that helped him recruit sailors. In 1668, he was selected as the commander of the buccaneers. In 1668, he would make some daring maneuvers off Lake Maracaibo, Venezuela, and make a getaway as his ships were trapped at the inlet. He ran a fire ship at the problem, *The Satisfaction,* and with grappling hooks locking into the Spanish ship, he had both blown up and burned. He even had his wood cutters carve out some silhouettes, so from a distance through a spy glass, it looked like his ship was manned: A tremendous tactical maneuver that made him the toast of the seas. He would become legend, and the stories got bigger and badder in the retelling.

In 1670, his crew captured Old Panama City, and Panama's governor ordered it to be burned to the ground. Everywhere Captain Morgan journeyed, he would use cruelty and torture to find out where the locals buried their gold and treasure. It worked, and they made a great haul of extra silver, gold, and precious gems. Morgan would abscond with much of the booty, but the pirates who served him got so rich that they didn't make a big deal of it. His buckoes would plunder Spain's Caribbean Colonies and run off with a load of Spanish gold *doubloons*, and chests filled with Spanish silver *pieces of eight*. The crew was *addled* with delight and couldn't wait to return to Port Royal to indulge in pleasure. Drink, eat, and go whoring. And Captain Morgan had the place ready to serve.

Did Morgan know that the English had inked a treaty, the Treaty of Madrid, with Spain before his last raid? He went for the loot anyway, and when he returned to Port Royal, he was ordered to England to be tried. History doesn't record the conversation with King Charles II, but I think the Swashbuckler told him some embellished stories, and how Jamaica was a bustling place and then showed him some of the loot. Wouldn't you know it? All was well, and the king didn't punish him, or discipline him. He knighted Henry Morgan. He was now "Sir Henry Morgan" and became the Lieutenant Governor of Jamaica. If you ever want to know why so many of us go the way of *scurvy pirate flesh*? It is because it works. Or so we think.

The French called this swashbuckler a *flibustier;* the Dutch called him a *zee-roover* (sea pirate), and the Spanish called him a *pirata*. Indeed, Morgan was a brilliant tactician, motivator, schemer, and businessman. He understood people really well and knew how we all can cave in to *scurvy pirate flesh*. This scourge got the best of him, too. Morgan would return to Port Royal and set up shop as the Lieutenant Governor. He ensured that Port Royal was protected with five forts by the bay. And everyone there was happy to be in business. Shoot fire, it was now the wealthiest city in the world. And soon it would be regarded as the wickedest.

The swashbuckler wasn't happy with everything. A writer and historian—a Dutch, Flemish, or French man named Alexandre Exquemelin who had sailed with Hank—was writing stories about him that didn't put him in the best light, accusing him of various offenses and torture.

Henry wasn't happy about this report. He successfully sued for libel, although reliable reports indicated that torture was practiced in the raid upon Portobelo in Panama. It seems as if the rich and the powerful get to write the history books. Do you think a few *pieces of eight* and gold *doubloons* were exchanged for this revisionist history? The Swashbuckler believed that image was everything and that money could buy you love.

Chew on This: Isaiah 53:6 says, "All we like sheep have gone astray; we have turned every one to his own way" (KJV). How do you see this independent streak in Captain Morgan? In his crew? In you?

Slavery

Captain Henry Morgan had the tiger by the tail with a downhill tug. He was recently knighted by King Charles II and appointed as Lieutenant Governor of Jamaica. This was his invitation: his right to go back to the island and become rich and powerful.

He understood human nature. The British loved tea, and he knew that Jamaican sugarcane would sweeten it up. The trade winds were going to be blowing in his favor. He also observed how the sailing people craved the taste of spiced rum, and it took a ton of sugarcane to make this hooch. Sugarcane grew easily on this sun-kissed island of wood and water. The loamy soil, enriched by volcanic ash, made this the perfect cash crop for him. In a few short years, he would develop three large sugarcane plantations and was in big business. International trade!

Growing sugarcane, harvesting it, and refining the sugarcane is a labor-intensive proposition. But this, too, was no problem for the conniving captain. More than 90% of the enslaved African peoples were delivered to the Caribbean and to South America. Captain Morgan purchased them like he would any commodity. He acquired 131 of these human beings and put them to work on his sugar plantations for cheap. There wasn't anything he couldn't own, even people.

Captain Lieutenant Governor Morgan is an example of *scurvy pirate flesh.* The Bible speaks of this condition as idolatry, and this man was an idolater (the 9 P's of Identity Idolatry: position/power, prestige, popularity, possessions, physical appearance, pleasure, performance, philosophy, and the past.) Morgan used his position as Lieutenant Governor to acquire valuable and productive land for his purposes. I am sure he called in all kinds of favors to get what he wanted. As the Lieutenant Governor, he had the English laws and the courts to back him up. He knew how to play the game, and he used his power to his benefit. Isn't it interesting how the powerful have ways of getting rich?

In the early 1690s, the population of Port Royal was from 6500–10,000 people. Of those, 2,500 were precious human beings owned as slaves, purchased from African kings as a commodity. They were often traded for furniture, firearms, metal goods (iron bars, brass bracelets, copper rods, pots, pans and kettles), textiles (mostly cloth), and alcohol.

The Royal African Company had slave ships that would voyage to West Africa to pick up recently purchased slaves to boost the local economy. They shipped more enslaved Africans to the Americas than any other country.

Therefore, Morgan had a cheap, steady, and ready supply of labor to make his sugar. In no time, he boasted of owning three sugar plantations and probably a couple hundred slaves to do the back-breaking work. He had a real "cash crop" he could use to *hornswoggle* his customers and live rich and free as a *freebooter.*

They would sweat as they chopped the sugarcane and burned the sugar out of those stalks. There was no end in sight for their supply as the thirst for rum and sweetener for tea knew no bounds. Henry had a "tiger by the tail," and the trade winds were blowing strong.

The deep-water harbor of Port Royal was making Henry's pockets deep and heavy with loot. Shoot fire, he rarely had to raid anymore, as all the business was coming to him, and the "royalty" in London were craving his "slave-sweetened" sugar. He had it going. He was making bank all the way around. The port was busy, and it is where the sailing men wanted to be. The trading was easy. A patron could have whatever they wanted as long as they paid the price. For sure, the captain made sure their appetites would be satisfied if they could pay the price. What could go wrong?

African slaves were transported by various world powers, and some of these precious human beings ended up in Port Royal. The following estimates show the weight and magnitude of this horrible trade. For example: Portugal/Brazil received 5,848,265 slaves during the 1501–1866 time period; Britain, 3,259,440; France, 1,381,404; Spain/Uruguay, 1,061,525; Netherlands, 554,336; USA, 305,326; Denmark, 111,041. By estimate, there were 46.2% to Brazil/Portugal; 22% to the British West Indies (one-half of which went to Jamaica). The remaining slaves were shipped to France, Spain, Netherlands, Denmark, and other places in the world. It is estimated that 3% of the slaves traded in this time period landed in the USA.[1]

Chew on This: Seeing people as a commodity seems to be real evil. How has this been a blight on our world? How is this a clear example of moral depravity?

1 Compiled from Brightwork Research & Analysis and Statista.

How did Henry Morgan exploit human nature to make himself rich? What is it about humans that would motivate them to sell human beings? (See Romans 3:23; 6:23.)

Note: Read *Pirate Greed*, *Real Spirituality*, and *Barnacles* to understand how human beings are capable of making *sharkbait* of other human beings to benefit themselves.

Hope Is a Floatation Device

Captain Henry Morgan was the brash, handlebar-mustached Lieutenant Governor of Jamaica. He gained success by trusting in himself and relying on his instincts, carnal as they were. He made tons of decisions, and they were all business decisions, even the ones that took lives and harmed people. He knew that *dead men tell no tales*, and he lived a "winner takes all" philosophy.

Morgan never allowed a *cockswain* or a writer to undercut him, question him, or tell their side of the story. He was a *freebooter* at heart and would amass huge worldly wealth by raiding, pillaging, killing, and rewriting stories to suit his purposes. He got rich by recruiting and influencing pirates to do his bidding. He always made sure that he took more than his share of the prize.

On the strong backs of African slaves, he farmed his plantations and developed a lucrative cash business. To Morgan it didn't matter if it were gold and silver stolen from Spanish ships and Spain's coastal cities, he always found a way to put money in his pocket. Shoot fire, he even made Port Royal into a turnpike, as he made *booty* coming and going. The trade winds would bring in fresh business, and he would stock those ships with sugar that he processed on his plantations and send it to England where those tea lovers would spoon it into their tea. One wonders if he ever felt as if he had enough.

The swashbuckler left nothing to chance. He had no place for hope—or for that matter, faith—or love. His confidence was in himself, and there is no evidence that he ever placed his faith in God. Don't forget he intentionally sank his own ship, the *Satisfaction* to save his own skin. Think of the irony of this. By taking matters into his own hands, he became one of the wealthiest people this world has ever known. He was making a killing in trade, by running Port Royal, and by having productive plantations. *Begad,* he had the power and the control of Jamaica as its duly appointed Lieutenant Governor.

But, did he have hope? Did he ever ponder the purpose of life? Or ask where God fits in to all of this? Or did he just take the bull by the horns and bully his way through life?

Tim and Esther had very little of what this world offers. But they felt like they were the richest people in the world. They had just experienced a beautiful honeymoon at the Blue Bay on this lush island, a paradise of wood and water. Tim had been shanghaied by pirate types and was forced into conscripted labor on the *Adventurer.* He didn't know how to swim. When he was on that wretched ship, he winced in fear every time he looked out on the unforgiving sea. During this honeymoon, Tim taught himself how to swim and built himself up while swimming almost every day. Esther would sit by their tent which they made from worn-out canvas sails taken from the *Adventurer* and watch her handsome husband exercise in the Blue Bay by swimming. She would be thinking through the Scriptures, writing a song, knitting, or doodling. She was happy to have so much love in her life.

They had a glorious time together. Their hope is in God, and they made meditating on the Holy Scriptures, singing spiritual songs, and prayer an integral part of their relationship. Their hearts beat as one, and, together, they are pumped full of joy. Gratitude is big to Tim and Esther; they want God to know how much they appreciate His watch and care for them. They were so thankful to God for giving them to each other, this time, this place, and a calling to fulfill. With this much hope and the promises of God, they are filled with a sense of purpose.

Incidentally, Esther's mother, Lily, was on a slave ship bound for Central America, when it broke down outside Port Royal. It needed repairs, and to get by, Lily would prepare peppers, oranges, bananas, lemons, and beans. She would arrange them in her basket and make her way to the bay and sell them to people on the dock. Hungry people were coming off ships. The men craved fresh fruits and vegetables as they were woefully tired of stale tack, and especially tired of soggy tack.

Her winsome smile and beautiful spirit caught Peter's eye and made his heart go pitter-patter. In no time, his heart was captivated by her. He felt it was God's will for him to leave the Franciscans, where he was a monk and had given his vows to live a life of service.

They married, and they were very happy to have this special love in their lives. They were living life to the full, fulfilling their mission by making disciples of the people God was bringing to them. With their relationship in full bloom, Lily became pregnant. They were thrilled to start a family. Tragedy struck when Lily gave birth to Esther; Lily died by bleeding to death.

Peter grieved for a good while, but he faithfully kept his vows to live a life of service, and he poured himself into raising beautiful Esther. He taught her the Scriptures and introduced her to singing. Like her mother, Esther had a precious spirit and a beautiful countenance. She also possessed a heaven-blessed gift of singing. Her tone and the sound of her voice was truly angelic. She sought to honor God with this gift. Peter would seek to build a community of believers in Jesus, but even as a little girl, the people were thrilled by her singing. God used this precious little girl and her sweet voice and spirit to minister His grace to these island-bound people. People came to their fellowship to hear this little girl sing and to learn Bible lessons from Peter.

When Tim arrived in Port Royal on the *Adventurer*, he and his Christian friend, Chase, had a serendipitous encounter with Peter. Soon they were meeting daily to discuss the Scriptures and to deal with the questions Tim was wrestling with. Tim grew up in London in a Christian home. He was part of a church community. He worked at Chauncey's Tavern cleaning and such to help his family financially, when he was knocked in the head with a hammer blow and shanghaied on to this ship.

This was a brutal experience for Tim. He was introduced to sinning that he had never known before. He felt as if all his innocence was gone, and the influence of pirate types like Pug and Brutus was dementing his mind. Tim wrestled with the dark and depressing memories from the ship. His own *scurvy pirate flesh* had even made him doubt that he could or should have a marriage relationship with Esther.

There were lots of experiences on that ship that contributed to him feeling insecure. But when he met Chase, and they together studied the Scriptures, Tim was buoyed by Chase's faith, God's promises, and Chase's commitment to him. Tim had pages of Scripture he lifted from the family Bible in his pocket. This was more than a crutch to him; it was life to him. With Chase they prayed and began to hope in God and believe Him for a future which Tim thought had been sunk at sea. Tim was a blond, naïve, English young man who was forced to grow up faster than one should. Peter really enjoyed helping Tim and Chase grow in their faith. Peter had a small farm and asked Tim to help him with it.

While out on the plot hoeing and working the land, Tim heard a beautiful voice singing Christian songs. He was mesmerized and had to move closer. Seeing what looked like a slave girl working, they began to chat and enjoyed working together. He would learn that her name was Esther, and, to his surprise, Peter would introduce Tim to his daughter. Tim was quickly smitten by her spirit and her beauty. He couldn't take his eyes off her and was enthralled by her beautiful and shapely figure. Soon they would be shanghaied by love. Papa Peter would take them through premarital Bible studies, and they would experience a white-waterfall wedding under King's Falls. They exchanged Christian vows and wore a strand of three cords united as one in the Lord. They were off to a great start.

Often Tim would miss his family, and they (Tim, Esther, and Papa Peter) would talk about it. Papa Peter especially knew what it was like to have a loss in life. But now, Tim was part of a new family and community. He just wished that his London family knew about him and how blessed he was. He had sent letters back on the ships, but he understood how unreliable these wretched people on these unreliable ships were.

While on their honeymoon, Tim and Esther discussed their plans for family and ministry. They agreed that both were the natural overflow of their love for God and each other. Their honeymoon was a grace-quest, and they poured themselves into trying to contemplate and understand the wonderful grace of God. Having thought and prayed about this grace, they were hoping and believing that grace would be their foundation and motivation for a life of ministry service.

During their time of premarital counseling with Papa Peter, they were given some favorite passages to study. Second Corinthians, Chapter 4 had captivated their hearts. It was filled with hope and purpose.

To return back to Port Royal, they took a big risk by selling their handmade raft that Tim built with Nick (Neckbeard), whom he also led into a relationship with Jesus. They took the proceeds of this sale and purchased tickets to the other side of the island where Port Royal was located. This was a risk for Tim because his previous experiencc on a ship made him leery to try again. Esther thought it would be fun, and, by being occupied with each other, they were faring all right.

On the *Rendezvous*, they met a wonderful chap named "Steward Steve." He quickly responded to their Christian faith, and together they enjoyed fellowship. Tim was open about his fears, and Steward Steve did his best to calm him. Tim asked Steve, if he were to be thrown overboard, how would he be rescued? Steve pointed out a hemp rope with many sealed gourds attached to it. He said, “This is a life preserver; it will keep you afloat, while we come to rescue you.” Tim was confused, but Esther explained that all he would need to do is trust in the life preserver, and it would keep him afloat.

She went on to share, “It is like our hope in God. Hope is a floatation device.”

Tim responded, “I know that God is the God of all hope.”

Esther smiled and said, “Yes, God’s love calms our fears and makes us secure.”

Esther, like her father, was always making little sermons out of life’s stuff. Tim just let her explain, and as he was listening. He said, “I get it: Hope is a confident expectation about the future.”

Esther sang out, “Glory, Glory, Glory!”

Tim laughed and commented, “We will live open and clear lives before God and each other, knowing that hope in God is like those sealed gourds. Hope in God will keep us afloat.”

Esther said, “We are unsinkable!”

Tim chuckled and said, “I guess you are right; I never thought of faith and hope like that.”

Esther said, "I like hearing you think I am right!" She went on and said, "Satan will try to get us to think dark and gloomy things, even fearing death, but God is for us."

Tim nodded his agreement and chimed, "We must do our part, by constantly having God renew our minds, in the current of grace. His love is like a river that can empower us and give us good thoughts. By nature, I don't always think the highest and best thoughts."

Esther was thrilled with Tim's comment and her smile affirmed him. She said, "*Ahoy*, that is a beautiful picture of God's grace. We do need His help to keep our hearts and minds fixed on Him."

Tim was daydreaming and was reflecting back on hearing Esther sing to him in the garden. Esther poked him and asked, "Tim what are you thinking about?"

Tim smiled and said, "I was thinking about meeting you in the garden for the first time. Your singing drew me to you, but even more beautiful, these simple Scripture songs draw me to God. This is a blessed way to get out of my *scurvy pirate flesh*."

Esther blushed and commented, "These precious songs remind us that Jesus is Lord. He is totally committed to us, and we are His servants."

Tim said, "That is deep, but true. I love that about you."

Esther continued, "It all comes back to those sealed gourds: we have hope. We are to BASK in hope and in the glory to come. The righteous are radiant, because Christ is in our hearts and seen on our faces."

Tim said, "But, to be honest, I often feel weak, like a fragile jar of clay."

Esther intoned, "Yes, jars of clay that contain the treasure, the Light of Christ in us."

Tim laughed, "Yes, you always have an insight that brightens me up." They hugged and kissed and reflected on the days to come.

The couple is excited to arrive in Port Royal and see Papa, Chase, and Clay and were hoping Nick would be there, too. But Steward Steve pointed out the obvious: the *Rendezvous* was in the doldrums and was standing still. The wind went and hid, and they were stuck in the placid waters in a slow drift toward the shore line.

Tim commented, "It is not the gale, but the set of the sail; but if there is no wind, we are stuck."

Esther said, "You have good word-pictures."

Tim said, "I heard that one from Papa."

Esther said, "Sounds like him. I guess we won't be home till tomorrow morning; that is if we catch some wind."

Tim said, "Everything is in God's time. I remember how disgruntled those pirates got on the *Adventurer*. We can't control the wind, but they wanted to. They weren't happy unless they were on the hunt and raiding for treasure. They needed adrenaline in their veins and wind in their sails."

Esther, "Yes, they were looking for love, but in the wrong place. Love wasn't home in their hearts."

Tim replied, "True beans, I know our new ministry will be challenging, too. Like the wind, we can't change anyone's life. Port Royal is a tough place. For sure resistance will be in our face."

Esther sighed, smiled, and recited, "But God raised Jesus from the dead. Wicked people, corrupt people, and an evil system killed Him. But God raised Him."

Tim affirmed, "Hope does float."

Esther said, "I have a confident expectation about our future. Hope is a floatation device."

Chew on This: According to 2 Corinthians 4:4,7, what do you think the treasure is in the jar of clay? How does this passage realistically deal with the struggles in our everyday lives? How were the sealed gourds a life preserver that gave Tim hope? How is God the "God of all hope to you" (review Romans 15:13)? We face many fears in this life. How then does having a life preserver give you hope? What can you do to "cast your anxiety onto the Lord" and experience hope and peace (see 1 Peter 5:6–7)? How does hope make you unsinkable?

White Picket Fences and Window Flower Boxes

Steward Steve and the crew of the *Rendezvous* are stir-crazy.

The wind stayed home today and the masts are limp. They are nervous because pirates could attack, maim, pillage, and loot from any direction. They could be hiding in a cove in canoes, or from out at sea. Being in the *doldrums* is an unsafe situation either out at sea, or on the couch. Tim was prone to want to be on firm ground.

Tim and Esther are not worried about their future. They are thinking about seeing Papa, Chase, Clay, and Earl again. They are hoping Nick (Neckbeard) will show up, so they can continue sharing the Word with him. Their conversation is chock-full of optimism, as they plan for their ministry in Port Royal. In a real way, Tim is acknowledging that he has much to learn about helping people in a spiritual way. Though he came from a good church community in London, he has never been a leader, and he is curious about how to reach and build up people in the Christian faith.

Having been on the *Adventurer* with a band of filthy pirate types, Tim thinks his innocence is shot. Wondering if he has seen it all, at the ripe age of 20, he asks Esther, "What do you think we should do to begin to engage the people in town?"

Esther said, "I think my mother had a good way by providing fruit and vegetables to the people and the newbies."

Tim replied, "I really did like getting my hands dirty and working with you in the garden."

Esther chimed in, "It is a spiritual exercise; you know God is a gardener."

Tim laughed, "Your insights amaze me; no wonder it is a delightful work to do."

Gazing out at the ocean, they look into each other's eyes and smile. Esther winks and says, "After all, our relationship began to bloom in Papa's garden. Papa taught often about how our responsibility is given to us by God in the Genesis account, to tend His garden." Tim didn't hear the last part of her comment, because he was blushing and laughing with joy remembering how their relationship bloomed in the garden.

He answered, "Gardening is good work; it is important to produce goods and provide services if we are to have the respect of the people."

Esther nodded her agreement and added, "We can't expect people to just show up at our church services. By taking fruit and vegetables to them, they can get to know us, and we can get to know them. Our work is a bridge into their lives."

Tim was impressed with Esther's understanding about work and how it is a way to do life with people. He is gawking and suggests, "You know, work communicates. It lets people know we want to serve them, and it lets them know we are not merely takers."

Esther beamed her approval and said, "Nor are we merely talkers."

Tim said, 'Thanks, that, too. People need food, and we like working with God to grow it, with the soil and moisture He provides."

Esther agreed, "He even had the volcanoes lay down some good soil, and there is plenty of sunshine."

Tim smiled and said, "This nature setting is amazing. We will bask in the sunshine and work in the garden. Sounds like a good plan."

Esther took Tim's hand and said, "People need food and spiritual food, too."

Tim agreed and added, "We will plant beans, potatoes, peppers, maize, melons, berries, and carrots."

Esther said, "I am hungry for some fresh food. And don't forget all the sweet fruit the trees provide: banana, mangoes, and avocados."

Tim said, "And with a steak, I'd be really satisfied."

Esther said, "Is food all you think about?"

Tim said, "No, you know what I am thinking about?"

Esther was blushing in her beautiful bronze skin, and chided, "You are thinking about the glory of God, huh!"

Tim chuckled, and said, "Our gardening business will help us reach out to the taverns and the hotels. This will be our way to be a friend of sinners, just as Jesus did."

Esther sighed, "Tim, that is really a good plan."

The *Rendezvous* was picking up speed, and the sails were billowing with the breeze. Steward Steve came by and said, "We should be in Port Royal by midday." The crew and the cruisers were happy to know that they would arrive at a safe time. Everyone was aware of Port Royal in the night: It has a reputation. Yet, most on board couldn't wait to *splice the main brace.*

Esther reckoned that Port Royalists would be pleased to offload plantains, mangoes, and bananas. Then they would load up sugar, cotton, and wood to send on the relaunch to London. The ship was encouraged and looking forward to the activity in Port Royal. This place was famous for its hospitality, entertainment, gambling, food, and drink. These guys would use any happening as an excuse to party hearty. It is called revelry, a party spirit. Not to mention all the sexual amusement on tap, the place was an adrenaline rush with all sorts of sensual stimuli.

Tim and Esther, with new excitement, returned to their previous conversation about business, outreach, and ministry in Port Royal. They were in agreement about their business ideas and were delighted to see how business could facilitate their ministry hopes. Esther said, “This is more than a business idea; it is part of a ministry strategy. It will be about building relationships and planting the seeds of the Gospel.”

Tim laughed, “See, it is just like gardening.” Esther just beamed.

After a moment of contemplation, she said, “It will be our bridge to the people on the bay and to those on the dock.”

Tim said, “Yes, it will have to be to the people who have made Port Royal their home and somehow to the strangers just passing through.”

From a distance, they could see some of the stations that guarded the Port. Captain Morgan had five of them set up to protect the bay. Steward Steve had run up a friendly flag to alert the “gatekeepers” of their friendly intentions. Esther was looking across the bay to the buildings; several of them were of fancy English Tudor design with shutters, flower boxes, and white picket fences.

She said to Tim, “I just love the stately look of these proper buildings. They look so nice and inviting.”

Steward Steve had overheard her comment and said, “That is just a façade. Port Royal is a wicked and dangerous place. You cannot tell a book by its cover. Be very careful.”

Tim and Esther realized that for a moment Steve didn’t understand that they were familiar with the area.

Because Esther had grown up around the bay and had been around people that Papa was ministering to made her very aware of the situation.

Tim said, “Pirates fly false flags to get what they want, and people put up false fronts just like these places.”

Esther responded, “I wasn’t judging the contents. I just said I like the white picket fences, the flowers in the window boxes, and this English style of building.”

Tim reached for her hand and said, “I think we know what we are going back to. There will be debauchery in the streets, drunkenness, and an orgy happening. You should hear how they talk about the whores.”

Esther laughed, “I have even heard the whores talk, but I refer to think of them as people made in God’s image.”

Tim replied, “We just need to consider how Jesus came to save sinners and was a friend of sinners.”

Esther agreed, lamenting, “They only know how to do evil all the time. They are dead in their sins.”

Tim reflexively responded, “That is the right attitude.”

Esther continued, “Let’s not forget that, while we were yet sinners, Jesus died for us.”

Tim chimed, “I know, but for the grace of God, I am where I am. I am also learning about who I am in Christ.”

Esther said, "I can just hear Papa talk about wearing the CROWN. You know he is right."

Tim said, "He made it simple ... we 'wear the CROWN and help others wear the CROWN'."

Esther nodded her agreement and said, "Let's not lose sight of the glory of God, as He will change lives, from glory to glory."

Tim said, "I wish I had the faith to believe that change can happen. You have heard me talk about Pug and Brutus. They were beastly more than human."

Esther opined, "I know. I know! People can be bad, and we are downright depraved apart from Christ."

Tim was bent on talking more and more about how evil Pug and Brutus are. Esther cut him off saying, "That is in the past. We will consider people as we think of the garden."

Tim said, "What?"

Esther said, "You know, till up the dark black dirt; take an ugly 'dead' seed and plant it; tend to it; water; cultivate; pull the weeds around it; then add sunshine. In time, the beauty of a green shoot and a pretty flower will sprout. The fruit will follow. This is how God does His best stuff."

Tim, shaking his head, said, "You are your daddy's daughter. He is always making those comparisons."

Esther said, "They stick with me, but they do give a positive and sunny outlook."

Tim affirmed, “You have a good way with words.”

Esther retorted, “Papa is a good teacher.”

Tim said, “That is for sure.”

Esther was gazing toward the bay as the *Rendezvous* was moving closer in to Port Royal. She lifted her head and said, “Our light will shine bright, in this dark place.”

Tim, looking out on the sea said, “We will be active in sharing our faith.”

Esther said, “We will learn about all the good things we have from God. He will give us the grace to help people.”

Tim said, “Yes, we trust Him. They are dead and don’t know it, dumb but don’t think it, deaf and don’t hear it, blind and don’t see it.”

Esther said, “You are good with words. How can they hear without a preacher and without God anointing them to believe?”

Tim said, “It seems desperate, but God is the God of hope.”

Esther said, “Yes, He is, and only He can raise the dead.”

Tim laughed and said, “I will keep these thoughts on the front of my mind.”

Esther said, “Even though I like white picket fences and pretty flower boxes! And, look, do you see the chapel and hear the bells?”

Tim said, “Wow, if I didn’t know better, I’d think we are entering heaven.” Looking at the other ships docked in the harbor, he said, “We are like those ships. They look good in the harbor, but that is not what they are for.”

Esther said, “You are like Papa, too. Maybe that is why I like you?” She continued, “Yes, we have an idea of what we are getting into. We are going to establish a mission, right next to the gates of hell. We will bloom where God plants us.”

Tim said, “I know my *scurvy pirate flesh* yearns for the easy life. But I am willing, and thankful, to take up my cross.” Esther leaned in for a hug and then began to sing:

“Lord, make me an instrument of your peace:

Where there is hatred, let me show love;

Where there is offense, pardon;

Where there is doubt, faith;

Where there is despair, hope;

Where there is darkness, light;

Where there is sadness, joy.

O Divine Master,

Grant that I may not so much seek to be consoled,

As to console;

To be understood as to understand;

To be loved as to love.

To know that in dying one is raised to eternal life;

Lord, make me a current of your grace."[2]

Steward Steve gave them a hug and a good word, "*Godspeed,* go with God." They thanked him and gave him the last of their *pieces of eight* as a gratuity. Without incident, the *Rendezvous* pulled into dock. As soon as the ropes were tied to the mooring, a man yelled *gangway,* and the passengers hurried off. The crew had some work yet to do.

There were cheery ovations from the townspeople, and the shopkeepers were there to greet and point the way to their establishments. They did have to step around some drunk people strewn out on the way across the dock. People were hanging out of the windows and making cackle calls. Tim and Esther had no one there to greet them. The people were eagerly looking for a tavern, to indulge in beer, grog, rum, and wine. Happy to be on solid ground again, or so they think.

Chew on This: Why is it that we want the easy life? This couple knew they were called to "take up their cross" (Matthew 16:24). What does that mean to you? What impresses you about Jesus leaving heaven and doing the hard stuff? What would have been the

2 Attributed to Saint Francis of Assisi.

most difficult things for Jesus to do after leaving heaven and coming to Earth? What costs were Tim and Esther counting as they returned to Port Royal? In Mark 10:43–45, we read that we are called to be servants and to lay down our lives. How do you think this is a good example for anyone who aspires to be involved in ministry? What blessings flow into the Christian who is active in sharing their faith (see Philemon v.6; Romans 10:8–21)?

Community of Encouragement

Having some meaningful good-byes to the crew of the *Rendezvous*, Tim and Esther now have the arduous task of making their way back home. All that they own is in their pack, and Tim is proud to carry it on his back. They spent every last *piece of eight* they had on their honeymoon and are completely broke except for faith, hope, and love.

They remembered how they enjoyed riding the Rio Grande on a raft they made with Nick's (Neckbeard) help. They had a beautiful and wonderfully sensual honeymoon in their tent made of an old sail from the *Adventurer,* at the dreamy setting of the Blue Bay. At the moment, they are not feeling unsinkable, as they are weighed down with present and future concerns. Getting off the dock will be a real relief.

Their first challenge is to traverse the dock strewn with drunks and get past the establishments that are beckoning for their attention. It is a good thing their loot is kaput and so are they. Tim and Esther can't wait to see Papa again, but they also are dead tired, as it is almost impossible to sleep on the ship. Once they made it past the taverns and boarding houses and hotels, they walk past Breeze's Café and immediately poke their noses in just to smell the fresh baked goods and to wave at Wendolyn. Tim and Esther look into each other's eyes, smile and agree that they would really enjoy some scones slathered with orange marmalade. Tim is craving his English tea. They will have to somehow refill their money bag before they can enjoy these simple pleasures.

Having come to the end of the boardwalk—a half circle that fronts the shops and borders the land of the Port Royal Harbor Bay—they now have to descend a big ditch and make it up a slippery slope of gravel, shale, sand, and limestone. They thought they were trying to climb a ditch of marbles. There is very little traction, but to get to Papa's home, they hand-in-hand help each other gain footing and make their way up to what is considered a plateau. When the couple is on solid ground again, Esther lets out a "whew," and Tim answers, "Yes, we are almost home." That acknowledgement brought joy to Esther, just knowing that her man was regarding this place as home.

On the rutted gravel road that leads to Papa's place, they look back out toward the bay and gaze at the *Rendezvous*. They pause and give thanks to God for how He faithfully brought them this far and for the experiences He has given them to deepen their relationship with each other and with Him. To catch their breath, they sit on a large piece of limestone and reflect upon their journey in life to this point.

Tim says to Esther, "I so love you. I can hardly believe we are here, not just at this place, but how God has brought us together."

Esther, with delight, replies, "I can't believe we are married because it has all happened so fast."

Tim said, "Our relationship is a beautiful love story. Who would think that I would get shanghaied in London, be conscripted by pirate types, and make a friend like Chase who saved me in many ways?"

Esther said, "Praise God from whom all blessings flow. What those meant for evil, God used for good. I am so happy God gave you a friend like Chase who met you at your time of need."

Tim affirmed, "I could have been destroyed except for the grace of God. If Chase weren't there, it was curtains for me. I remember distinctly how he met me at the rail and let me know he was for me and was a Christian, too."

Esther giggled and said, "And to think that God had Papa meet you in the chapel and help you both understand the Scriptures."

Tim nodding affirmatively said, "What a life saver! Papa helped me so much! He had a Scripture verse for everything. He really understands and then he gave you to me."

Esther and Tim embraced and kissed. While holding hands, Esther said, "How many people get to have marriage counseling? Who would think that on this island I would find a man who aspires to purity and values me as a woman?"

Shaking his head, Tim said, "I haven't thought of it that way. This really is ordained. God has led us by His hand. I am so grateful to have you. Papa's marriage talks helped me a lot. I think back to the *Adventurer* and remember thinking that my life was over. It was only evil all the time. Now I did learn some bad things about my soul, but God saved me again and again."

Esther said, "Wonderful, isn't it! Amid this decadent place, God has given us something beautiful. He grows beautiful roses on heaps of dung. Our White River Falls wedding at King's Waterfall was more beautiful than even royalty could have. I feel like a real princess."

Tim said, "I will cherish you riding on the raft down the Rio Grande and feeling like the Queen of Sheba."

Esther laughed and said, "That was fun! We felt so free, floating, and riding the current of God's grace."

Tim said, "I always want you to feel this way. After all, Papa always talks about 'wearing the CROWN'."

Esther laughed and said, "Yes, he does. Our relationship has really come together."

Without speaking, yet vividly thinking, Tim was caught smirking and Esther just knew what was on Tim's mind. Tim was in a gaze, daydreaming about the kiss behind the waterfall and the super sensual and beautiful sexual experiences he shared with Esther under the covers of the worn-out sails from the *Adventure*.

Esther is now rolling her eyes and says, "Tim, snap out of it."

Tim just smiles and says, "I sure love you. You are a treasure, and you are beautiful."

Esther ah's and says, "We need to get ready to face our community." Tim agreed.

Hugging and kissing, Tim and Esther reckon that they are happy to have had this pause. They are excited to get home and see Papa again, but they needed a clear view from Mount Perspective. Realizing that on the *Rendezvous*, they talked so much about their future plans that they hardly know what to do with the present. They refocus their attention on how important it is to re-engage with old friends and family. They really have missed their community and can't wait to see them again. When a couple marries, they leave and cleave, but then they must get out of just building their self and their relationship and seek to help others.

This thought is further developed as Esther said, "Tim, see the ships (as they, from this vantage point, look back at the Port Royal Harbor)?"

Tim says, "Yes, it is an impressive picture."

Esther declares, "Yes, it is. Those ships look good in the harbor, but that is not what they are for."

Tim is astounded and says, "You always make spiritual lessons out of life stuff. You are your daddy's daughter."

Esther laughed and blurted, "I knew you would get a kick out of this observation, but it is true, huh?"

Tim said, "I get it; it is about you and me, too."

Esther beamed with delight and replied, "We enjoyed our honeymoon, but as a couple, we have a purpose. I think we will fulfill it by building community."

Their thought was now being taken off self, and they were now thinking and talking about the relationships that so mattered to them. Tim was asking Esther to help him remember some of the names of the townspeople that had connection to her family (Papa).

The walk from here is less than a quarter mile, a bit uphill, but will be traversed quickly. They review the names. Some of the locals, Esther has known from her childhood, while others recently landed there. Esther asks, "Do you remember Malinda? Wendolyn? Clay? Earl?"

Tim has to admit, "You know, the only ones I really remember are Chase and Nick, and, of course, Papa."

Esther asks, "Why didn't you remember the others?"

Tim confesses, "I was only thinking about you and myself."

When they arrive at the house, Esther just walks right in and shouts, "Papa, we are home. Papa, we are home." There was no reply, so they reckon that, since they have been away, Papa would be out tending the garden. It was now late into the afternoon, and there must have been lots to do because during the heat, most people take a siesta.

They walk toward the garden, which is in full bloom. Sure enough, there at the far end is Papa working with a hoe in hand. They shout in unison, "Papa, Papa." In one smooth motion, Papa drops his hoe and throws his wide-brimmed Panama hat up into the air and runs toward his children, smiling from ear-to-ear and shouting, "Happy day!" He hugs Esther, and then Tim, and says, "Welcome home! I missed you."

Picking up his hat and his hoe, they then walk toward the house and reminisce about their honeymoon adventure. Papa wanted to know everything to a point. In general, he wanted to know about their experience. Inwardly, Papa was happy to see that they still liked each other and were in love. After all, he officiated the marriage ceremony and led them the in exchanging their vows.

As they sip sweet tea, Papa fills them in on their community. He says, "This little church has been a community of encouragement," telling them that they all regularly prayed for them. He said, "They will all be happy to see you."

Papa announced, "We have a new member of our group, even a couple of new additions. Nick has joined us. He talked about meeting you on the river and helping you build the raft. He is growing in his faith, so good seed has been planted in his soul."

Tim and Esther were happy to hear the news and said, "Wonderful, praise the Lord!"

Papa agreed and said, "And Chase has a new parrot, a bird named Frieda, and she rides on his shoulder. He is trying to get her to say, 'Praise the Lord,' but all she says is, 'Ah, old fart'." They all had a good laugh.

Chew on This: According to Hebrews 10:24–25, we are to encourage one another to love and to do good deeds. We are not to forsake meeting together as some do. But we are to encourage one another as the day is drawing near. Why then do you think Tim and Esther are so concerned about building community? Is this a primary thing Jesus wants to do? Is community something He wants all of us to be thinking about and working for? What can God accomplish in our lives through community, which He can't do if we fly solo?

Tim's Epiphany About Community

Tim and Esther were so tired, that they decided to spend the evening in Papa Peter's home. They were eager to meet up with old friends and fellowship, but the time on the ship made Tim so uneasy, and Esther agreed to stay home and talk with Papa into the evening. They enjoyed talking over Papa Peter's "practical pointers for producing personal relationships from gardening." This is also known as the premarital counseling the couple received before their honeymoon in the Blue Bay.

The laughter was only hushed by their yawns. But Tim and Esther let Papa know how profoundly his lessons were regarding their relationship. Tim couldn't believe how prophetic his words were to them. And he was amazed at how gardening proved to be a wonderful way to explain how to grow a healthy relationship. They agreed that the lesson on cultivation was especially helpful as Tim confessed that there was a time during the honeymoon when he allowed his heart to harden, and he isolated himself. He agreed that it took God and Esther's patience and understanding to work on his heart, as a hoe does to the dirt.

Tim was dozing off in Esther's bed, but Papa and Esther stayed up talking about all the amending God did to the soil of their relationship. Esther was impressed with how the Word of God gave them guidance and how singing Scripture-filled songs renewed their minds. Papa was really encouraged and mentioned that this is what he prayed for. His hope was that their honeymoon would provide a solid foundation for them to build their relationship.

Esther mentioned that being away from community was difficult. She said, “It was good to be alone together. We had some healthy activity, swimming, exploring, talking, and reading together, but we missed the stimulation of Christian fellowship.”

Papa was happy to hear how she was looking at things. He was especially encouraged to know the priority this young couple was giving to the Word of God. Esther stated that the Word of God met them over and over again at their time of need. While laughing, Esther said, “We also found a number of weeds that were encroaching on our relationship, and we needed God’s help to pull them out of our relationship.”

Papa just nodded and mentioned that that is the normal Christian life. He said, “We will always be weeding and watering, if we want to grow.”

Esther laughed and said, “I think the difficulties are proving to be fertilizer as the dead fish we cultivate into the soil in our garden.”

Papa said, “Isn’t it interesting about what God uses as fertilizer? Some of the most unpleasant and stinky stuff is the best fertilizer for our garden and for our lives.” He continued, “I am so happy you are home safe; I am happy that God used this experience to help you grow up in our faith more and more. My joy is seeing you grow and have joy."

Esther said, "Papa I am very happy, and I am glad to be home."

Papa smiled and said, "And I happy to see that you love each other and are walking with Jesus."

Esther snuggled into her bed with Tim; he just rolled over because he was fast asleep. Waking up the next morning, Tim felt awkward and weird being in Esther's bed and Papa's home. While lying in bed, he had a vision of taking the outcropping of limestones from the fields and pulling them out, shaping them, and using them as the foundation of a new home and gathering place. This vision brought joy and energy to Tim. He could just see a beautiful place, with a patio, gardens, kitchen, bedroom, and a place for fellowship. He was so excited about this vision, that he walked toward the garden and was looking at all these natural outcroppings and the garden, the beautiful stones that were imbedded in the hills and fields, there for the taking. And by pulling them out, they would have even more cleared land to farm. He had no idea how to dislodge them and haul them, but he was excited.

While standing in the middle of the garden with the ocean in the background, he noticed that there was just a little haze today and an assortment of trees bordering the garden. The smells are intoxicating, and Tim is taking it all in to his senses. Tim is walking in circle with arms outstretched and is amazed with the beauty of this setting and how rich the soil is. This place is a perfect garden setting, and Tim, in his mind, is picturing string beans, and a patch for melons, a place for peppers, and carrots, and a field of maize.

While picturing in his mind a bountiful garden, he is dazzled by a vision. Seemingly from out of nowhere, he hears waltz music and sees the limestones rising up from the ground and off the hillsides, glorying in their irregular shapes and jagged edges. The stones begin to dance to the music. It is as if they turn happy and lift their "hands" and rhythmically waltz their way to Papa's end of the garden, where they are—in an organized fashion—set into walls that make a beautiful foundation for their home and gathering place. Piece after piece are assembled, as if by a team of master masons; yet, effortlessly and without any struggles with gravity, they are placed and make for a beautiful and solid structure. The jagged edges and irregular shapes and sizes—and in a variety of colors—gave structure to the vision. Supernaturally, these stones lock into place and make for a "living" wall that will endure any hurricane or earthquake. This rhythmic movement happens to the beat of the inspired waltz music.

All Tim can do is check himself to see if he is really awake and if he is truly standing in the garden. He smells the fresh citrus scents wafting off the trees and knows he is alive. As he gathers himself, he realizes that he has just been entertained. He laughs and offers praise to God and hears God in heaven laughing and enjoying the moment. Tim looks to heaven and just smiles; this was a special moment that he will always cherish with God. But, will he tell anyone? Or just cherish the moment?

He retraces his steps and realizes that these limestones will make a wonderful foundation for their home and gathering place and reckons that somehow God will do it. Even though he and Esther have an agreement to be open and transparent with each other, Tim thinks it is good to downplay this experience and keep it between God and him, though he does see clearly their home and gathering place.

Tim's joy is abounding and both Esther and Papa wonder what is up with Tim. He is like Moses when he came down from the mountain and had to cover his radiant face. Tim is thankful that God, who is both infinite and personal, chose to share this special interlude to encourage him. Tim is grateful and full of joy.

The big event of the day is the Bible study and fellowship night. Papa will be teaching on First Thessalonians, Chapter 5. When they gather at the little chapel, the greetings are heartfelt and joyous. Everyone is happy to see Tim and Esther. Chase is there with his new friend Frieda, and Wyndolyn and Clay are there, too. And to their delight, Nick shows up and gives Tim and Esther a big hug. There might have been a dozen or so folks there for the study.

Papa is beaming and expresses his happiness to have the newlyweds back home. Like a good pastor, he tends to his flock by focusing them on the Good Book. It takes a good while to call the "irregular stones," that is the group, together because they are so locked in on sharing life and their experiences together.

It is difficult to study the Word of God because only Papa has a handwritten portion of this text. Printing presses are a new thing, and they are waiting for the day when a complete Bible will be available to them. Tim has the printed pages of the book of Ephesians he keeps in his pocket. But Papa just can't wait to get a freshly printed Bible or a New Testament. But what he has, he faithfully delivers to these believers. He does the best he can trying to teach and explain because most of the people can't read, so he knows he has to build trust with everyone.

He begins by saying, "This chapter of First Thessalonians, Chapter 5, is about the end of the age. It is a preparation passage to get us ready for Christ's return. Jesus is coming back, and we must be ready for Him when He returns. Jesus will return unexpectedly. People will be all about peace and safety, like a bunch of pirates just taking care of themselves. Then disaster will fall! Like a pregnant woman, she knows her baby is coming, but not when. We must stay ready.

"We are not in the dark. Jesus has told us He is coming, and He is going to come like a thief in the night. For some, this will be a terrible thing, but for us, this will be glorious. It is glorious for us because we are not children of the night; we are children of the light. Therefore, we are not in darkness. We can be ready. We are to always be wearing the armor of light, of faith, and of love. This way, we are confident. We know where we stand, and He knows us. He is coming for us. We are saved. We don't have to fear judgment, because His love for us makes us secure. I ask you, what are we to do while we wait?"

Chase said, "Encourage one another."

Papa cheered, "That is right, and that is what it says (Papa points to the page)." Chase was pleased and the group cheered his answer. Papa continued, "Yes, we are to build each other up while we wait for Jesus to return."

Tim asked, "Papa, what does it mean to wait for His return?"

Papa said, "Good question. Certainly it doesn't mean do nothing."

Then he explained, "I think we are to be building relationships, with the body of Christ and the needy world around us. Always be doing good and showing love. Remember: They will know we are Christ followers by our love. So, keep praying, watch over our hearts by being thankful, walk in the Spirit. We need to be reminded to stay away from evil."

Papa was leading the group in a prayer, where he basically prayed the lesson that he just taught over the people.

Tim lifts up his head looks around and sees the people in the little group as the "living stones," he observed earlier in the day. He bows his head and offers his own thank-you prayer to God. And he lifts his head, opens his eyes, and now he sees a beautiful bouquet of flowers. The group is now a beautiful bouquet of colorful and bountiful types of flowers. The scent is amazing—the picture is captivating: each individual with a unique personality. One unified bouquet; yet, each flower is so different. Unity without uniformity, a special "community." Tim bows his head again, and he is getting the message to his human spirit that this group will become a beautiful flower bed, that has no fear of being overtaken by weeds because these flowers crowd out weeds.

Best of all, these flowers cannot be contained by one flower bed. They begin to encroach on the entire community.

Tim is overwhelmed by the Bible lesson, but is especially encouraged by the personal applications God has imparted to him with these glimpses. This is a new and unusual experience for Tim. But he cherishes it in his heart. His epiphany is that he has a responsibility to work with God to develop this community of encouragement. Until now, he has only received the benefits of his family back home in London, their church congregation, and the blessings of Chase, Papa, Esther, and this small fellowship. It is now clear to Tim; he is to be a builder and shoulder responsibility. He is beginning to understand: to whom much has been given, much is being asked.

Chew on This: How is the body of Christ a living wall (a wall of "living stones," 1 Peter 2:5)? What is irregular, uneven, and jagged about you? How does the Holy Spirit help you to fit in the "living wall?" How do we become a beautiful bouquet of flowers? How can we crowd out weeds? What would be weeds in our fellowship/ bouquet? How does God make flowers beautiful? How does he make us beautiful (review John 13:34–35)?

Tend the Garden

Sid Huston

Are you in the desert?
And looking for purpose?

Wondering and longing
Hoping for direction?

Look no further than Genesis 2
And you will know what to do

A little bit of prose
The good book shows how it is supposed to go

In 2:15, the beautiful garden was filled with life
Then sin made it full of strife

There were two trees central to the story
One is holy and the other gory

Knowledge of good and evil, do not despise
For it is filled with lies

The glorious "tree of life"
This is the only way to be wise

Adam and eve showed their self-will
And God let them see they were
alone, naked, and chilled

However, He let them know they were not forgotten
Asking them to "tend His garden"

We must return to the tree of life
It is found in the cross of Christ

In this tree where Jesus died
This is where we discover life

Where we experience true purpose
Delight in God and be in His service

The cross has two bars
Vertical and horizontal

God reaches down to us
And we reach out to others

In this outreach, our love will hearten
For there is unending purpose
found in tending His garden

Where the vertical and horizontal meet
This is a place of holy confluence

And we begin to live lives of godly influence
Any other way is incongruence

Faith and works flow together
As we practice His presence

This is like a river glorious
Showing that God is with us

In this mighty current of grace
Glory is seen on your face

So, in His garden

His grace I apprehend

As I think about my family
For them I will always contend

Think of the poor
And to the Lord lend
Think of the oppressed
To the weak defend

Thinking about racism
These relationships I will mend

Think of the lost
Say, "God, here am I, send"

Think of your true meaning
Know, Jesus is the beginning and the end

All of this is discovered in His implicit command
Live in fellowship with Him
And His garden tend

The Rut of Routine

Life was good for Tim. He was finding his calling, and he had a home and a family that he loved. His only concern is for his family back home in London Town. But he has sent several letters back chronicling his story and assuring them of his safety. He hopes they have received the parcel, and he is anxious about a return letter. He wants them to know that his new wife is beautiful, kind, nice, and filled with grace and wisdom. And she can sing.

The couple have been home from their honeymoon for a couple of months now. The garden is now caught up. They have learned to "plant by the moon." So now that it is the beginning of May, the squash and pumpkins have been planted. They are proud of their work, and, once again, Esther is at one end of the garden this evening and Tim at the other. Tim is thrilled in his human spirit to hear Esther sing.

"Time, precious time

God makes everything beautiful in His time

Eternity is in our hearts

He alone has set the time

It is up to us to join Him

A time to be born

And a time to go home

A time to plant

And a time to gather

Everything in His time

His Spirit gives the rhythm

A time to speak

And a time not to speak

A time to lament

And a time to repent

A time to embrace

And a time for space

A time to rip

And a time to stitch

A time to hug

Time, precious time

God makes everything beautiful in His time."

Tim was delighting in the beautiful music coming from Esther, her sweet spirit, and amazing voice. And more, he was interested in the words. He walked toward Esther with the hoe in his hand. He cheered her performance, and then he asked, "Where did you get that song?"

Esther said, "I made it up, but I think it is in the Bible. Solomon said there is a time for everything under heaven."

Tim said, "Yes, I agree, but I am out of balance. We have been working so hard to get the garden caught up and looking for work, so we can pay for our dreams."

Esther, nodding her head in agreement, said, "I agree. We need to get on Jamaica time and get in a steady routine we can live with."

Tim asked, "What is 'Jamaica time,' and what is a routine?"

Esther laughed and asked, "You don't know of Jamaica time?"

Tim leaned against the hoe and said, "I have no idea."

Esther said, "We are not on a clock; we are event-oriented and not time-oriented."

Tim said, "What?"

Esther explained, "When we have church, we get started when the Spirit leads, and we go for as long as our spirits need. You Londoners—British folks—set your clocks. We don't have them and are not run by them. We'd much rather get in the rhythm of the day, the season, and the weather. Why fight it?"

Tim replied, "Good point, explains a lot. But what is routine?"

Esther thought for a while and said, "I think a routine is a habit, a habit of regular activity, a consistent way to go about our day, or our week."

Tim said, "That sounds good, but what goes into that habit of regular activity?"

Esther moved close to him and hugged his neck and said, "You know, time for us to walk, to read, to play, to go to church, and to pray, and, of course, we have work to do."

Tim replied, "I could use some of that."

Esther smiled and said, "Me, too."

Tim asked, "How do we get it? We just seem to work, work, work, and some worship and meet with people."

Esther responded, "I agree. We need to get some discipline into our lives. Let's talk about what is most important to us and then set up our habits of regular activities that way."

Tim said, "I want time with you."

Esther smiled, giggled, and said, "That sounds good to me."

Tim said, "I mean Jamaican time with you."

Esther laughed and said, "Yes, but we had the most beautiful honeymoon at the Blue Bay. We lived that way."

Tim said, “Yeah, *arrr.* And I liked it.”

Together they agreed to have breakfast at Breeze’s Café and dive in to developing regular habits and organizing their activities. The next morning, before their day ran away from them, they went to Breeze’s Café. Esther had a *piece of eight* she had stowed away. They both knew that money—or making some money—was something they needed to build into their habits.

But what was most important to them was knowing they were fully alive, rich, and free. They just wanted that honeymoon feeling again, and since being back in Port Royal, they were cramped. They loved everyone, each other, family, and community, but something was draining the joy out of their lives, and it was time for change.

Tim was enjoying his English tea, and Esther was nibbling on a scone. She looked up at Tim and said, “Try this scone.” Tim tried to bite into it. Esther smiled and asked, “Think I can do better?”

Tim said, “Oh, yes, you can.”

Then Esther asked, “Do you think I should ask Wyndolyn for a job here?”

Tim said, “Baking is something you love to do. You *are* good at it, so why not?” The couple continued talking about what needed to be in their routine. They made a mental list of all the priorities they had, and it seemed long, especially long when they considered that they both needed to secure “day” jobs.

They talked about time for prayer and devotions, the garden, the Christian community, and "together" time for them. They reckoned that God knew all that needed to be done, and they committed their list to Him. They really didn't know how to sort it out, but they knew if they committed their way to Him, He would sort things out. They both admitted that the honeymoon was nice by not having responsibilities, but just having a lazy relaxing day just to enjoy God and each other in nature was delightful. But now they are in the "real world," and a really wicked world at that.

Esther mentioned, "I know it seems daunting to try to organize our lives, but God is a God of order, so it can be done. I believe the result of our attempt to discipline our time will result in freedom."

Tim said, "Yes, I think so, and also impact. I am afraid that when we are with people, we are so hurried, and life change takes time."

Esther cheered, "I thought I was the only one who felt that way."

Tim smiled and chimed, "We just need to bloom where we are planted. I have heard that somewhere."

Esther said, "That is one of Papa's sayings."

Tim laughed, "I knew it wasn't original."

They both felt better having talked about things, but they also knew that it would take work and regular discipline to form some new habits. And, to add to it, Esther was working up the gumption to talk with Wyndolyn.

The couple said a quick prayer, and then Esther sought Wyndolyn, who was standing behind the counter. The kitchen was in the back (detached to keep the heat away), and she spent her day walking from the counter to the outdoor kitchen. Esther got her attention and asked if she needed help. Wyndolyn said it depended on how good she was and gave her a challenge. Esther wanted to bake some scones because she knew she was good at those. But Wendolyn said, "The sailing men love pie, and if you can make a delicious mango pie, I might have a place for you." Esther agreed to her challenge and was determined to bring a delicious mango pie to the café for consumption.

Tim rejoiced at the news, because he knew how good Esther's baking was. Esther wasn't so sure. Tim said, "You are going to have to go home and practice, and I will be the tester. I will see if I can get Papa and Chase to help, too." Esther was excited about the opportunity and wanted to do her best. She got really quiet, and Tim noticed. He said, "Baby, what is wrong?"

Esther said, "We were just talking about our use of time and our routine, and now I need to bake pies."

Tim said, "I will help with what I can, and remember, the rut of routine is the groove of grace."

Esther couldn't hold back her laughter and blurted, "Yes, and there is a time for everything under heaven."

Tim said, "It is tough, but I think I can make some time to test mango pie."

Esther rolled her eyes and began to hum her song: "Time, precious time. God makes everything beautiful in His time."

Chew on This: How can the "rut of routine" become a groove for grace? Does God give the grace for us to sort out our priorities? Does He give us the energy and strength to do the things we need to accomplish in our daily lives? How can Nehemiah 8:10 be the key to our daily grind? Read Ecclesiastes, Chapter 3 and ask, is there really a time for everything under heaven? What is it about God that makes Him the Lord of even the time? Do you think He can make everything beautiful in His time? Why? Why not? (King Solomon thought much about time in Ecclesiastes 3.)

It's All Fun and Games

Port Royal is always loud, rowdy, and obnoxious. The people, both the men and women, are mostly licentious, gluttonous, and always wanting more, and they think they deserve it. They act like they paid the price just by showing up. Pirates say, "It is all fun and games until someone gets an eyepatch."

While sitting around a table at Breeze's Café, Esther was trying to get Wendolyn's attention and drop off a couple of fresh mango pies. She was hoping they would sell fast today, so Wendolyn would hire her to provide pies and other baked goods. Papa, Tim, and Chase thought for sure they would fly off the counter because they tasted so good.

Esther didn't want anyone to know about her secret ingredients of nutmeg, cinnamon, sugarcane, lemon, cornstarch, and butter (plenty). She also shredded some coconut to top it off. She wanted to keep this recipe to herself. She has sourced these ingredients locally. In her mind, this recipe was job security.

The men with Frieda, the parrot, who was riding on Chase's shoulder, were just enjoying some tea and lemon drink and a couple of scones. But what they enjoyed the most was their conversation. It is good to sit and talk with friends about life and to stay in touch.

Papa especially liked the opportunity to keep short accounts with Tim, as he wanted to make sure things were all right with Esther, and that he was learning by discussing the ministry. They enjoyed talking about how Jesus changed the world with a dozen "irregular people." Papa was convinced that, this way, God gets more glory. He even found it ironic to note that these people would turn the world upside down and would be considered as saints, and people the world wasn't worthy of.

At the front of the café was a free-swinging door, and three men dressed in white linen tunics walked in. Now, there was an uneasy quiet in the café. Chase rolled his eyes and directed their gazes to the new guests in religious garb.

All three of these men were wearing long cassocks with waist belts of different colors. Papa could tell that Tim and Chase were put off by these vestments and the feeling of religion. After all, Papa was always teaching about a relationship with God—and not religion—but rather by being alive, rich, and free in Christ. The feeling that Tim and Chase got from these uniforms was totally other. But they followed Papa's lead and remained cordial.

Papa smiled and nodded his head toward them, as he had met them before on the dock as they frequented the area to strike up conversations with the people. Papa quietly mentioned to Tim and Chase that there was a time when he, too, wore a gray habit with a hood when he was a Franciscan monk. He said, "Their cassock is a symbol of peace, purity, and order. Certainly, something this Port could use more of. When I wore the habit, it was a reminder to me that I belonged to Jesus and was committed to Christ and to my brothers. It was simple and ingrained in me that my life was to be a simple life of service. Remember that Francesco, Saint Francis of Assisi, didn't wear sandals because he so wanted to relate with Jesus who left everything in heaven to come to this earth."

Tim said, "Going barefoot would be rough here."

Chase agreed, then nodded and affirmed Tim. But their awkward feelings were palpable.

Papa greeted these priests with a "good day" blessing and a smile. It wasn't long before they took their seats at the table next to them. In the contingent was Braden Newell, a rector at the Church of England parish. Thomas Brower was an assistant pastor of a smaller Church of England congregation in the area. And there was Oswald McNeil, the superintendent of these priests.

Introductions were made, and Papa shared that he was trying to lead a little flock of Christ followers, too. The men all had encouraging looks on their faces and then Reverend Newell spoke up, "It is happy to see that you are following Jesus in this unlikely place."

Papa said, "We were just talking about how Jesus left the comforts of heaven to come to this desperate place."

Reverend Newell agreed and then continued, "We regularly meet to have some fellowship and to encourage each other in the work here in Port Royal. This is a very difficult place, as few people seem to have any thoughts of God."

Oswald McNeil and Thomas Brower chimed in and affirmed that ministry here is tough.

Thomas said, “It is even difficult to strike up a conversation because people think we want something from them. We just want to give them the love of Jesus.”

Tim said, “Do you think your cassock turns them off?”

Oswald nodded and said, “There are times when it is a barrier, but it is always good for people to know what we are about. I used to resent this tunic, but now it reminds me to represent Jesus and to be set apart.”

Papa said, “Amen, brother. I used to be a Franciscan monk, and I wore a gray habit. It set me apart, but that is what the word holy means, to be ‘set apart’.”

Reverend McNeil chimed in, “This place is anything but holy.

Frieda squawked, “Holy, Holy, Holy!”

Chase laughed and said, “That is a first. But “holy” is such a good word. It is who we are. When I first got here, I was so full of s*curvy pirate flesh*— that is what we call the sin element and pirate-like tendencies in us—I, too, just wanted to eat, drink, and be merry. And live as if I were going to die tomorrow.”

Thomas laughed and said, “I think that is true of all of us, for all have sinned and fallen short of God’s glory.”

Then Oswald replied, “But for the grace of God.”

Reverend McNeil continued, “We usually have Reverend Emmanuel Heath meet with us, but for some reason, he didn’t make it today. I hope he is all right.”

Papa said “I think I have met him; he is a real gregarious chap.”

Braden said, “That man can preach.”

And Thomas asked, “Have you heard him sing?”

Reverend McNeil said, “Shoot fire, he can sing! We should just set him up and turn him loose; he has a heavenly gift.”

Tim spoke right up and said, “My wife, Esther, has a beautiful voice, too, and she loves to sing Scripture-filled songs.”

Papa smiled and said, “How good and pleasant it is for brothers to dwell together in unity.”

Reverend McNeil declared, “And we need to pray. This place is full of evil.”

Chase responded, “I have heard that there are recent deaths because of alcohol poisoning. The “kill-devil” [early name for rum in the 17th century] is appropriately named, huh!”

Thomas spoke right up, “The thief comes to kill, steal, and destroy.”

Tim affirmed, “But Jesus came to give us life, abundantly.”

Oswald said, "That is the good news, but there is bad news here. Last week a man was out walking the dock swinging his cutlass, and he lopped off a man's arm for no reason. Blunderbuss guns have been shot into crowds, and a person died for just being in the wrong place. So many men and the women are suffering with sexually transmitted diseases. They have the clap (gonorrhea) and syphilis."

Braden declared, "It is a shame. This place is so beautiful, so blessed with resources, but the sinfulness of man has made it a den of sin and shame!"

Reverend McNeil ranted, "These people have no fear of God. They are gluttons. They are drunkards; the men just want the strumpets. There is always fighting in the taverns. People hallucinate; they are always saying crazy things, and they black out and lose their bag of loot. Then their revenge motive kicks in, and, before you know, it is dangerous. I fear that this place will be snuffed out. How much can God put up with? These evil people have no future."

Papa stated, "But for the grace and mercy of God they do. We need the Holy Spirit to bring about repentance, and we will be there to help the people turn around. No one is righteous without Jesus. People on their own are pirates. They are not smart, and they are unworthy of air and water. No one does well without God."

Reverend McNeil continued, "These pirates make this place a den of iniquity. They stink, and this place could become an open grave. They couldn't care less than they do. Destruction is everywhere. There is no respect for God or others. They lurk and look to ambush. They are pirates. That is who they are."

Papa remarked, "I agree; yet, they don't see it. It is like they have a patch on each eye."

Thomas Brower laughed and then spoke up, "They are Epicureans!"

Everyone looked at each other as if Thomas just served them a word stew.

Papa asked, "What is an 'epi' what?"

Thomas said, "Epicurean. Epicurus was a Greek philosopher.

Tim replied, "Now, I am curious."

Thomas said, "I was able to study the Greek philosophers, you know, Plato, Socrates, and Epicurus. These people here seem to hold to his ideas."

Papa said, "Really, I would like to know more, as I haven't been able to study that."

Reverend McNeil had gotten up and returned to the table with a piece of mango pie. "This is the best pie I have ever tasted."

Papa, Tim, and Chase smiled.

Papa looked at the others and said, "Get a piece before it is gone."

Esther was sitting by the door and Papa nodded his head toward her. She smiled back. Wendolyn came in to visit with the men, and McNeil raved about the pie. Wendolyn looked to the counter, and there was only one piece left. Braden really wanted it so badly. The men had such a good time of fellowship, that they agreed to meet again in a few days to continue the conversation and learn more about Epicurus. They were now, all curious.

On the way back to Papa Peter's house, Tim and Chase were interested to see what Papa thought about their discussion.

Chase asked, "Peter, what do you think about what the religious leaders had to say?"

Papa said, "I am happy to see that they understand the depravity here in Port Royal and cared so deeply. And I am glad God has given us an understanding of the CROWN. The scurvy pirates we see come off those boats are really completely different from what we know of our identity found in Christ: Righteousness, Order, Worship and Nobility. It occurs to me that the wickedness we see is anti-Christ, unrighteousness, chaos, self-centeredness, and ignoble. I mean they have low or no character. Their behavior currents out of their identity, too. It is sad to see. But Jesus came to save sinners and give people His righteous identity.

Tim answered, "*Shiver me timbers.* That is deep water, Papa."

Chew on This: In your opinion, why was Port Royal loud, obnoxious, dangerous, and deadly? Look up John 10:10 and see the comparison between Jesus' way of living and Satan's. What does Satan, the thief, come to do? Is it safe to say that Satan is the chief pirate? Why? Why not? Why were Tim and Chase put off about the religious garb worn by the ministers? How do you feel about that? What was Papa's experience that can help with understanding this? How is this an identity issue?

The ministers vented about how evil the people were. Was this venting redemptive? Why or why not? How did Papa Peter concur that the depravity they witnessed in Port Royal is really opposite of each letter in CROWN? Do you see this, too?

Epicureans in Port Royal?

Papa Peter, Chase, and Tim were interested in meeting with the religious leaders and talking about Epicureanism and Greek philosophy. They were intrigued by Thomas Brower's assertion that the sensual behavior they see here in the port was related to the philosophy espoused in epicurean philosophy. Papa wasn't so inclined, as he was of the persuasion that it was just plain old *scurvy pirate flesh* that explained the drunkenness, promiscuity, and gluttony they observe every day just going about their business.

Today, the word got to the religious leaders to meet after breakfast outside of Breeze's Café. Dr. Emmanuel Heath is the Anglican rector of Saint Paul's Church, which is just one block off the dock, the church with a large steeple. He was going to join the group with a civic leader and friend, John White, who was concerned about the mounting costs that the violence and drug use was costing the community. And not to mention the terrible reputation Port Royal had garnered around the West Indies, the Caribbean, and in the sailing world.

As the group gathered, there were happy greetings and comments about how much they appreciated their last meeting and how encouraged each one was to see such heartfelt concern for the souls of these lost people who traffic in Port Royal.

After a brief time of fellowship, Dr. Heath spoke right up, saying, "I am happy to join you today with Mr. White. My suggestion is that we go on a prayer walk up and down the boardwalk along the bay. Without being pharisaical and showy, we will be in an attitude of God-directed prayer, offering up to Him our sincere requests for the people we see, and the businesses and the ships we see in the port."

Tim mumbled to Chase that he thought the white linen cassocks were a bit showy.

"We know that our God—though He is unseen—is present here, and we desperately need His protection and transformation here."

The rest of the contingent were saying "Amen" and expressing their agreement. The group spun off and staggered their steps so as not to be a crowd. They naturally mixed with people they didn't know very well, just to get to know new brothers in the cause.

Thomas joined with Tim and Chase. And let's not forget Frieda, who was along for the ride, but was being quiet today. Papa Peter partnered with Dr. Heath and Mr. White. Oswald McNeil and Braden Newell picked up the rear.

As they were walking, Thomas pointed out the tavern titled, "The Sign of Bacchus." He whispered, "Later we will be talking about Epicureanism, and this tavern depicts what we will be talking about, as Bacchus is the Roman god of wine and earthly festivity [known as Dionysus in Greek mythology]. He was known for his sensual love of pleasure and getting his 'jollies.' He even endorsed being in a spirit of revelry and sensual behavior."

Tim responded in a muffled voice, "I had no idea where they got that name. I just thought they like to *splice the main brace.*"

Papa confirmed, "Behavior does current out of identity."

As Braden was looking around and pointing, he said, "Makes sense. Look at some of the other taverns' names: The Feathers, The Black Dog, The Cat and Fiddle, The Blue Anchor, The Sign of the Mermaid, The Green Dragon. Do you know what these names mean?

Oswald spoke right up, "The 'Cat and the Fiddle' is a nursery rhyme about a cow jumping over the moon. The 'Black Dog' is a sign of depression, sadness, or an omen of impending death, and the 'Mermaid' is about life and fertility and great imagination out at sea."

Chase said, "*Blimey me*! Mermaids are sexy things, argh!" Then he asked, "What do these names have to do with anything?"

Thomas answered, "It is about responding to emotions and feelings and getting your imaginations and pleasures satisfied while seeking tranquility."

Braden was mystified and was still gazing at the businesses on the dock. He mumbled, "What could a 'Blue Anchor' stand for?"

Oswald chimed in, "It has long been a symbol for 'staying put'; you know, not always chasing."

Tim responded, “I know when I was out at sea, I just wanted my feet on solid ground and to have a home.”

Thomas agreed, “I think that is a longing God puts in our hearts.”

Chase asked, “So what is with ‘Cheshire Cheese’?”

Dr. Heath laughed and said, “In London, it is a tasty cheese like cheddar.”

Tim commented, “It is really good.” Then he asked, “Does anyone know if ‘The Green Dragon’ term has any special meaning?”

Thomas said, “I think it has an Oriental meaning for being able to control the wind.”

Once again Tim commented, “I was so impressed with these sailing men who could take whatever wind they had and adjust their sails and get the ship to go where they wanted it to go. Papa always says, ‘It is not the gale; it is the set of the sails’.”

Dr. Heath nodded his affirmation and responded, “It is amazing, the power of the wind. We need the Holy Spirit, too, like wind blowing a revival into this port.”

Papa Peter wholeheartedly agreed, and the men broke out into a spontaneous prayer for the people in Port Royal. The men would see a man *addled* and sloshing drunk staggering down the street and pray for him or her. As they walked by the various establishments, they would pray for the proprietors and the patrons. They had to step over and around some completely inebriated people, who looked washed up on the dock like a dead fish on the rocks. A couple had recently died from alcohol poisoning. But they just kept addressing their concerns to heaven.

The bay area wasn't that big, just 40–50 acres and 2,000 buildings crammed in to host 6,000 and some odd number of people. All of this was built to provide all kinds of service to the sailing world. And, don't forget: It was guarded with 5–6 forts on a slit of 10–15 miles into the guarded bay that was protected by pirates for pirates. Mr. White knew full well what this haven was all about, and it is not a glimpse of heaven.

As the men continued to walk, talk, and pray, they walked by blacksmith shops, carpenter shops, tanners, tailors, hatters, upholsterers, painters, carvers, gunsmiths, knife dealers, net makers, and armorers. Not to mention the obvious evidence of slave and sex trading. There was a good amount of two- to three-story English-style mansions with bricks from London. The ships would load the brick in England and use it as ballast to steady their ship and build some beautiful buildings. The men met the folks of Port Royal and offered a kind greeting and quietly lifted their prayers for them to God. They prayed for their salvation mostly, but they also prayed for peace and safety, too.

When they returned to Breeze's Café, and after everyone was seated around the tables, Dr. Heath said, "I just want to see some semblance of religion here in Port Royal."

Papa Peter retorted, "I want to see what happened in Nineveh and revival."

Thomas stepped up and said, “I hope you have an idea of what I meant when I said there is an epicurean influence that has invaded this place.”

Tim jumped in and commented, “I noticed about every fourth building was a tavern or a brothel. Is that epicurean?”

Thomas responded, “Can you see that Epicureanism is a feeling-oriented and sensual philosophy?”

Chase joined in, “Having sailed, I see that all you want when you get off that wretched ship is good food to taste, good sex to feel like a man again, and clean fresh water to drink.”

Thomas responded, “Yes, Epicurus thought that a person could only really trust their feelings, so he developed a philosophy that was void of logic, reason, even science. Consequently, the followers of this philosophy were not motivated to study, explore, or achieve. All they did was medicate their psyche by pleasuring themselves, and the only effort they make is to seek tranquility. Do you see the connection to Port Royal now?”

Papa asked, “What did they think of God and Scripture?”

Thomas was eager to answer, “I think they are like deists.”

Tim jumped at the comment, “What is a ‘deist’?”

Thomas declared, “A person who thinks that there is a god, but God is impersonal, distant, and doesn’t care. The originator has stepped away from creation and allows things to operate as a wound-up clock."

Papa was incensed, "This is a sad belief. I was a follower of Saint Francis of Assisi. He taught about how personal God is and how intimate He is, always singing and preaching about the 'birds of the air,' the 'lilies of the field,' and how we mean so much more to Him and are in His deep care."

The brothers were in agreement and were "Amening" Papa's comments.

Thomas said, "Let me clarify a couple ideas found in epicurean philosophy. Because of this presupposition that 'god' doesn't care to be involved, therefore the aim of life is to abandon anything that makes demands on your life—such as responsibilities—just eat, drink, and make merry."

Chase asserted, "Somedays that sounds good to me. I see the gluttony, rest, and the carnality. My *scurvy pirate flesh* has those appetites."

The men laughed, and then they turned quiet.

Thomas continued, "In this philosophy, which means a man's idea, there is no definition or sense of sin and no fear of punishment. They even try to take all sense of fear out of their minds. I think they know that fear has to do with punishment, and they avoid these thoughts, as they would a storm."

Tim said, "I can see where Christianity would seem restricting, condemning, and having too much responsibility."

Papa was pleased with this response, "Bravo, young Tim! It really is a very selfish and sensual philosophy of life. I find nothing redemptive in it. It reduces life to self-satisfaction. Tranquility sounds nice, but there are tough times and rough waters that are unavoidable, and, worse, there is no service or sacrifice in this philosophy as I see it. And where is the hunger and thirst for righteousness? These people are just lofting at sea in serenity. What a waste."

Thomas nodded his agreement and said, "There are two words that sum up its essence: ataraxia and aponia. "Ataraxia" is tranquility and serenity, the place of freedom from fear. They avoid arguments at all costs and won't engage in politics as they think that causes stress. "Aponia" means freedom from suffering."

Papa said, "I get it. I just wish they would realize that God's perfect love casts out fear."

Thomas agreed, "Very good."

The other men affirmed with a "yes."

Then Thomas continued, "Aponia is the absence of bodily pain, often achieved by limiting or denying desires, and getting rid of fear. Their aim then is pleasure."

Chase said, "I see that it is a philosophy of avoidance and mellowing out. No wonder they smoke the weed."

Thomas stated, "Well done, Chase."

Tim responded, "I don't think they are all that tranquil; after all, they got all those gold doubloons by raiding and pillaging Spanish ships and coastal communities."

The men mostly nodded their agreement.

Braden and Oswald admitted that they were fascinated by the discussion and could see why Port Royal had such appeal to pirates.

Braden said, "This place is an epicurean delight because it is all about satisfying a man's feelings and his senses: sex, food, liquor, weed, rest, calm breezes, and relaxation. They want paradise."

Thomas said, "You are on to it."

Oswald agreed and mentioned, "I see why it is so attractive. It is an easy philosophy to buy in to. It makes no demands and allows one to justify a life of ease. After all, fighting the seas wears a man down. Persuading people to come to Christ is hard work."

Thomas said, "True."

Then Oswald burst out, "I could go for a piece of that mango pie and tea right now." The group laughed and clapped their agreement.

Papa was earnest and said, "The apostle Paul said, 'Don't let anyone capture you with empty philosophies and high-sounding nonsense.' This has been a good discussion."

The group agreed. Then Papa asked Dr. Heath to close their fellowship and discussion in prayer, and he did. In his prayer, he mentioned how Jesus gave us an example of self-sacrifice and laying down one's life.

Chew on This: In your opinion, how is Port Royal an epicurean delight? According to Colossians 2:8, how is this philosophy "empty"? Why isn't Christianity easy? Pleasure oriented? What does sacrifice have to do with love and a relationship with God? In Acts 17:18, the epicurean philosophers were mentioned. They thought the resurrection was a strange idea. Why would an epicurean think the resurrection strange?

Work Matters

Papa Peter, Esther, Tim, and Chase reflected on their conversations with the religious leaders in Port Royal. Papa was convinced the behaviors that plague the port are none other than *scurvy pirate flesh.* Tim and Chase thought it was an interesting discussion about Epicureanism, but agreed that a life of tranquility and serenity didn't even imitate God.

Chase pointed out that, in Creation, God worked for six days and then rested on the seventh. He mentioned God has a high value for work and modeled it. Esther was in agreement and said, "We are told to imitate God. He is our example on how to live this life."

Tim smiled and suggested, "We are called to follow in the footsteps of Jesus, and He came to do His father's work."

Papa said, "I think behavior currents out of identity. We wear the CROWN: Christ, Righteousness, Order, Worship, and Nobility. Their behavior is opposite the CROWN. What is going on here is anti-Christ, unrighteous, chaos, selfish and fleshly, and ignoble. They care nothing of the glory of God. They live to satisfy their fleshly appetites. That is Epicureanism plain and simple. I think it is good for us to just love everyone and be about doing the work God has put in front of us. Thinking about work, have you seen Earl and his prized steeds, Onyx and Ivory?"

Chase said, "Boy, howdy! Those are beautiful beasts of burden that do so much for this community."

Tim said, "I agree. They pull carriages, plows, wagons, and even ships when they need to be put in a spot."

Papa was talking about how useful they are, and Tim sparked with a smile and had an epiphany. In his mind he could see those horses pulling the irregular sandstones out of the farmland and even grading a foundation for the gathering place and home Tim and Esther are dreaming about. Tim just knew that he had to get to know Earl and see if he could work a deal.

Papa then tried to quote a passage from Proverbs 6 about work. He said, "Let's learn a lesson from ants: people are naturally lazy. So, go ahead and learn from their ways. We can become wise by watching ants. Though they don't have a prince or a governor or a superintendent to chide them into working, they work hard all the time, anyway. They gather food for the winter. But lazybones just roll over in their bed and sleep away their opportunity. We can fold our hands and lay down our heads, and then poverty will pounce on us like pirates raiding a ship."

Esther said, "I see where you get it Papa; you have such a strong work ethic."

Papa said, "Even Francesco [Saint Francis of Assisi] would sing about how it is happy to work and to do our work for the Lord. I even believe the reward for faithful service is more work. Don't we all want to hear Him say, 'Well done, my good and faithful servant'?"

Tim responded with joy, “I agree. There is joy in work.”

Esther said, “As long as we are doing our work for the Lord and remembering that He is our audience.”

Chase said, “Amen!” and Papa added, “Our work matters. We all can be a blessing to our community by finding and delivering good work. I will never forget meeting Lily on the dock. She was so beautiful in her simple dress and a basket filled with fruits and vegetables she had prepared. Her positive attitude about work was one of the things that attracted me to her.”

Tim said, “I have heard that a way to a man’s heart is through his stomach.” Esther gently elbowed him in the stomach.

Chase said, “You ought to know that Esther’s mango pies are a big hit at Breeze’s Café.”

Esther said, “I am happy to have a job. I enjoy it, but it is hard and hot work.”

Papa applauded, “I wish you could have seen your mother. She was so beautiful, and so industrious. I am so happy you have her nature.” Tim just beamed and grabbed for Esther’s hand.

This happy family finished out their day, and the next day, Tim was on a mission to go and meet Earl. He found him and Onyx and Ivory in a man’s garden, pulling out dead trees.

Tim watched with amazement as Earl would put the chain around the tree, and, on command, he let loose commands that were laced with colorful "pirate speak" and swear words. He didn't just say pull or dig. He said, "Onyx, you so-and-so, and Ivory you are a blankety-blank-blank." Words you would never want your mother to hear you say. But the horses responded with gusto. Onyx and Ivory would dig in, and with their muscular hind legs, they pulled—and then pop! The trees' roots and all were out of the ground. After they had done their work, they looked so proud, and Tim thought for sure they were smiling. Earl rewarded them with oats and water.

Tim stepped out and introduced himself, "I hear you are Earl and you have some magnificent steeds."

Earl smiled, cursed a bit, and said, "These are great work horses."

Tim asked, "How big are they?" Earl said, "Onyx the black one is 16 hands high and weighs 1,500 lbs. And Ivory is 18 hands high and weighs almost 2,000 lbs."

Tim said, "They do so much good work for our community."

Earl said, "They live to work, and they are happiest when they are working. Of course, I reward them well."

Tim asked, "How much can they pull?"

Earl said, "Tim, you ask a good question. Individually they can pull 8,000 lbs., but together they can pull 24,000 lbs."

Tim replied, "*Shiver me timbers*, that is amazing. Why do you think they can do so much more together?"

Earl said, "I think they are a bit competitive and do not want to let the other down. But it is true that we can get more done when we work together."

Tim responded and asked Earl, "That is why I am here. I wanted to see what it would cost to have you and your horses remove some irregular pieces of sandstones from our farmland and then use those stones to lay a foundation for a home and a gathering place."

Earl said, "I will come by your place and take a look. I will give you a bid for what it will cost."

Tim said, "That will be good. I don't have any money yet, but I am looking for work."

Earl asked if he knew Clay, a blacksmith on the far side of the bay. He mentioned that he had a difficult time finding good help.

Tim said, "I have heard about him; he is big and rough."

Earl said, "You can't read a book by the cover. He is a good man, speaks little, but does real good work and has a good business."

Tim replied, "I will go and meet him."

They shook hands. Tim was about to walk away, and then the horses were begging his attention, and Tim asked if he could pet them.

Earl said, "Better, yet, you can feed them."

While feeding them out of a wooden bucket, Tim asked, "What kind of horses are these?"

Earl answered, "I think Onyx is a Percheron, a kind of draft horse raised in western France. It has a solid black coat, and that is why I call her Onyx."

Tim asked, "And Ivory?"

Earl replied, "She is a Belgian Draft horse, known for being the strongest breed in the world."

Tim said, "I don't doubt it. I saw how they pulled those trees out, roots and all. They are muscular and powerful."

Earl said, "They are lovers: they love to work. They are smart, and, best of all, they love to please me."

Tim bobbed his head and then smarted off, "Then why did you use such abrasive language with them."

Earl laughed, "They know the sound of my voice, and when I get stern, they know that I mean business."

Tim mentioned, "They responded to you very well."

Earl said, "They know that I love them, too. They are gentle giants."

Tim asked, "What does that mean?"

Earl replied, "If we have a tough job, they can work all day. They are patient. They stay with it, and they are diligent."

Tim asked, "Does Papa know about your horses, where they are from, and what they are known for?"

Earl said, "I don't know."

Tim responded, "I will tell him because he will make a Bible lesson out of their work ethic. Say, Earl, have you ever come to our fellowship gatherings?"

Earl said, "I am not a religious sort. You heard me talk to the horses."

Tim answered, "Well, you are invited, and you would like our humble community. Some real people and an encouraging simple faith."

Earl said, "I will take that under consideration."

Seeing these steeds in action got Tim excited. He wasn't just excited about his conversation with Earl and learning about these wonderful, gentle, yet powerful giants. He was excited to know that the land could be cleared, and a gathering place could be built. There was a lot of work to do, but he just knew that if he could build a relationship with Earl, and if he had the money, he could get the job done. But how was he going to get the money? What work could he do to earn the loot to pay the bill to get the stones moved?

After all, a worker is worthy of a wage, and Earl has a lot of expenses to keep those horses well fed.

So, Tim sought out Papa and had a sit-down conversation and asked about who he thought he could work for and earn some good money and still pay attention to the gardening and building the church. He realized that, in reality, the garden wouldn't be productive for a while, and it wouldn't be really productive until the field is cleared and prepared.

While talking with Papa, Papa mentioned Clay the blacksmith. Tim intoned that Earl had mentioned Clay, too. Papa went on. He thought Clay ran an honest business, was a hard worker, and always had business. Ships always needed something repaired, and Clay was known throughout the islands as being a man who could repair and repurpose most anything made out of metal. Papa let Tim know that his shop was at the end of Lime Street, right close to the bay.

Tim was eager to go and meet Clay, but first, he just knew he needed to pray and talk with Esther about it. Tim had been learning to cast all of his anxieties upon the Lord and to ask God for anything in prayer. So, in a real natural conversation, as two people talking to each other, Tim laid his heart bare before God. He wished he could hear an audible voice, but, by faith, he knew God was listening, and that in a quiet way, God was communicating to his human spirit.

Esther was open to the idea. She especially liked the idea of walking to the bay together and thought it would be safer for her and hoped their schedules would work out. So, she, too, prayed for Tim to go and meet with Clay the blacksmith.

The next morning, right after the roosters crowed, Tim and Esther made their way to Breeze's Café. Tim carried the pies and the scones Esther had baked on her home oven. When Esther got to the café, she put on her apron and went right to work in the outdoor kitchen. To have a kitchen in the building would just be too hot.

Tim ordered a plate with cackle fruit with peppers, English muffins, and tea. This put Tim in a good mood, as this breakfast was one of his favorite things. Then he went behind the café. He and Esther said a prayer together, and he kissed her good-bye, as he began walking down Lime Street.

Tim was nervous, but when he got to Clay's blacksmith shop, his nervousness subsided. Clay, though shy, let out a hearty *ahoy* and asked Tim to hold the tongs so Clay could shape a metal bar that was hot from the hearth.

Tim couldn't believe Clay. Muscular, his shoulders and arms looked like the legs of Onyx and Ivory, the horses. His muscles were bulging. His wrists and forearms were covered with leather bands. Clay had a handkerchief covering his head and hair, as his hair was everywhere: on his shoulders, down his back, on his arms, and flowing out of the heavy leather apron that covered his chest and went to his knees. His dark brown beard had some red in it, making him look like a Viking warrior. It looked as if that was all he wore, as he didn't wear a shirt. He did wear short pants, but, like Esther in the outdoor kitchen, this shop got hot, as well. And Clay had to keep the hearth afire while he was shaping metal. So, at first glance, it looked like all he wore was an apron.

Tim was no slouch, and he held the tongs hard and fast, and, in just a minute, Clay was satisfied with his work.

Tim asked, “How would you have done that if I weren’t here to help?”

Clay answered, “Thanks for lending a hand. It is hard to do this work all by myself.”

Tim said, “Four hands are better than two.”

Clay said, “I could use some help. I haven’t been able to keep help.”

Tim said, “My name is Tim, and I am looking for work. Why is it so hard to find and keep good help?”

Clay said, “And I am Clay. Call me Clay. Many a man comes in here, and they claim to be a loyal worker, but they are not.”

Tim asked, “What seems to be the problem?”

Clay said, “Usually it is the hooch ... you know, the grog, rum, kill-devil, beer, and wine. Then it is the weed, and often it is sickness; lots of men get the crabs.”

Tim laughed, “I don’t suppose it’s the crabs in the Atlantic Ocean, huh!”

Clay said, “No, it’s in their britches. They get the itches and can’t work worth a darn. And some just can’t hack it. It is tough hard work, and you have to be strong.”

Tim flexed his pronounced bicep and said, "I am not nearly as strong as you, but I can hold my own. I don't drink. I am married, and I am faithful to my wife, and I would be faithful to you. So, I hope you would find me reliable."

Clay and Tim talked about a reasonable wage with some incentives and agreed that Tim would start work in the morning after he walked Esther to Breeze's Café.

Tim and Clay shook on it, and Tim left walking and leaping, praising God, grateful to have a job. He just knew that he could add value to Clay's life and maybe make a friend. For sure, he was going to learn some new skills to be productive and earn some loot, so he could do even more good.

He stopped by Breeze's Café to share the good news with Esther. He waited for her to be done with her work, and then they skipped their way home rejoicing. When they gathered for dinner, Tim was happy to share the good news with Papa Peter and Chase.

The group held hands and offered their thanks to God. They committed Tim's work and relationship with Clay to God, and they also prayed for Wyndolyn, who had given Esther the opportunity to serve through her baking. This was a happy time for this band of believers in Jesus.

Papa, never one to miss an opportunity to bring a lesson, shared, "I think the best way we can thank God for these work provisions is to do our work heartily as unto God. Our work matters."

Chew on This: In your opinion, does your work matter? If so, why? In your work, who is your real audience? Take a look at Colossians 3:23–24 and draw some priorities and attitudes we should bring into our work. Can you name three values that will improve your attitude regarding work?

What is the significance of God working? Does He still work? Why did Jesus come to work? What does it mean to do His work? How can your work life be God's work, too? What can you learn about work from the ants (Proverbs 6:6–10)? What can you learn about work from Earl's horses Onyx and Ivory? For example, when are they the happiest? How about you? What makes you happy regarding your work? How does your work matter? How can our work open up relationships for our personal gospel outreach? Why do you think "doing good" means so much to Tim?

Bloom Where You Are Planted

Tim was standing out in the field. From here he can see the sea and can't help but remember growing up in foggy London Town where everything is just a variety of shades of gray.

But, here in tropical Jamaica, the colors are vivid and the air is clear and fresh. Beautiful birds dart from flower to flower, and the colors scan the spectrum of a color wheel.

His story of working at Chauncey's Tavern and then getting shanghaied by pirates and waking up groggy on the *Adventurer* as a conscript still looms heavy in his mind. While charting his garden and standing in the field, he can't help but daydream and wonder what his life would have been and can hardly believe God has once again caused these things to work together for his good. He smiles, and his eyes twinkle, as he looks at Esther, who is putting beans in her basket. She is beautiful and a delightful person to share life with. With friends like Chase, a mentor like Papa, and a new job with Clay, life is good, really good.

Even though he is trying to sketch out a plan for the maize—melons, beans, and squash—he is gazing in amazement at the beauty of this island. He feels unworthy, but grateful and realizes that this setting is packed with heaven. The rich soil has been artfully amended with ash from the volcanoes that formed some of these glorious islands. Add in regular showers, sunshine, and sea breezes, this a lush and advantageous parcel to grow just about anything.

The lignum vitae, also known as "the tree of life," catches his eye, and he marvels at the little blue flowers that glisten with the sun's rays. These flowers pair with the orange flowers, yellowish-orange fruit, and dark green foliage from the wood blossom. Then, next to it, he sees a poinciana with gorgeous red, yellow, and orange flowers. It is a proud flower that fans its "feathers" and struts like a peacock. This thought makes Tim laugh.

He thinks, "Yep, even flowers can be proud and a bit arrogant like some people he knows." He scans the area and laughs again, as he thinks about the pretty love bush. Its small white flowers abound, as it climbs upon a tall blue mahoe tree almost 50 feet into the air. It makes a beautiful shawl. It occurs to him that this plant, though it is leafless, has pretty little bright multicolored flowers.

His eyes rise to the tree tops, and then he slowly looks down to see a bright red poinciana tree, dazzling his mind with red leaves and red flowers. It is stunning. The reds know no end, as underneath it are red poinsettias with glossy green leaves. Contrasted with the pink, yellow, and orange flailing petals from the blue mahoe, he has enjoyed a show here in paradise.

His thoughts soar Godward, as he declares, "God, only you can make a tree like this." Tim knows this is conversational praise, and it is becoming to Him. He likes it, because he senses in his human spirit that God does, too. He continues his gaze around the garden and invites Esther to join him in this time of praise. Together they enjoy the hibiscus with its large trumpet-bell flowers and the orchid growing on the bark of a tree. The fern is beautiful, as it cascades down the tree's trunk. There is the passion flower full of color: yellow, pink, white, and purple. Together they praise God with a word: "Amazing!"

Esther's favorite plant in the area is the turkey tangle fogfruit, an inviting groundcover with delicate white flowers. It makes her think of a royal wedding.

They are captivated by a flamenco vine that is standing alone and basking in the sun. They both realize that they, too, need to be like this flower, as there are times when one needs to stand alone.

The heliconia draws some laughter from the couple, as they agree that it has flanges and appendages like fingers that look like a crab's claw. Tim notices that some of them are red; others are orange, and some are yellow. They are only pollinated by the green hermit and the violet sabrewing hummingbirds that whirl and flutter, as they do their work and entertain Tim and Esther.

Esther quotes her father saying, "These beautiful flowers and trees all bloom where they are planted."

This was really good for Tim to hear because, from time to time, he gets in his own "London fog" and dwells on missing his family and wondering about what is going on back there. Yet, Esther's reminder here sparks joy, as he, too, wants to bloom where God has planted him. As they look at a passion flower, they hold hands and kiss, thinking how God has given them something just as beautiful in their love for each other.

As they walk toward home, they talk about how the rut of routine has become a groove of grace for them. They are gainfully employed and striking a balance with their relationship and their ministry to their community. They cherish the moment together.

Every morning, they enjoy their walk to Lime Street, where Tim kisses Esther good-bye for the day, and they give each other a blessing. Esther begins her work at Breeze's Café, and Tim joins Clay for work in his blacksmith shop. On these walks, they talk about everything that is on their minds. After Tim is done at the shop, he stops by the café for a cup of tea and waits for Esther. Then they walk back to Papa's place. When Tim is really hungry, they talk about what is for dinner. Tonight, Esther is going to fry codfish and cook it with tomatoes, onions, potatoes, and peppers. They will have some sliced mangoes and relax.

They siesta and wait for some cool breezes to refresh them, and then they head out to the garden to work some more. They do not fight the heat, because they have learned to just lay low when it is hot and make their work revolve around any bit of cool they can get.

This is their routine, but on Wednesday, they meet with their church community, and Papa leads in a Bible study. This is the highlight of their week, both the teaching and the fellowship. They value the people in their group and are trying to gather more. Esther has a few new friends at the café she is praying about inviting, and Tim is working on Clay.

At the end of each day, they try to think back about the "God-sightings" they experienced and commit their steps and relationships to the Lord. They both believe that God led them to each other, and even to their work. They pray for God to help them "bloom where they are planted."

The next day at dinnertime, they share this "bloom where you are planted" idea with Papa, and he likes it a lot. He says to Tim, "I think you are seeing that God has called you and appointed you to be here and to bear fruit."

Tim agreed and asked, "Where did that thought come from?"

Papa said, "I believe it is in the Gospel of John, Chapter 15, where Jesus speaks about the vine and the branches." They take some time to reflect on that passage and are once again amazed at how the Bible speaks to what they have been thinking and experiencing. Papa continued by saying, "I think the passage goes on to say that we are to bear fruit that brings the Father glory."

Esther chimes in saying, "That makes sense, as the flowers in the field do that naturally."

Papa, who is not one to waste a teachable moment, goes on, "God's first command in the Bible is to 'tend the garden.' There is a lot to tending a garden, such as clearing the land, cultivating the soil, collecting seed, planting seed, watering, pruning the trees and plants. We are even learning to fertilize with fish, and then we must harvest the crops and prepare them for market to sell them. There is a lot to do."

Tim said, "*Ahoy, matey*. You are telling me!"

Esther was paying attention, as she thinks this idea of blooming is on God's heart; after all, Jamaica is a beautiful garden. She asks, "What does it mean to bloom?"

Papa smiled and answered, "The seed germinates, and we see the green shoots coming up out of the soil. Then, with time and sunshine, there will be a bud on a branch, and, before long, it is a 'blooming' flower. And then the branch gets to 'bear' the fruit."

Tim asked, "Why did you speak louder about 'bear' the fruit?"

Papa cleared his throat, "Very good, Tim. We don't produce a thing. We simply abide in the vine, allow God's "SAP" (the Spirit and the Anointing) to flow, and the miracle of fruit happens. God causes this growth. We simply have the privilege of 'bearing' the fruit. But first we must bloom."

Esther commented, "I have heard you speak of this before. Does it have to do with basking in the sunshine of God's love?"

Papa rejoiced and said, "*Ahoy*, you got it! We lift our hearts in praise and BASK in His love and we grow. His light produces life in us. It is *His* life in us. SAP flow is the Spirit and the Anointing, which is the ability to live out of His identity. All this is released into our lives as we Praise him. The SAP flows."

Tim said, “It all comes together. This BASK idea is the key: Bless, Ask, Stay, Know. I have even seen you practice the motions.”

Papa said, “It is a wonderful way to find balance. Speaking of balance and blooming, some of the brothers in our order of Franciscans read about Saint Francis de Sales, a bishop from Geneva.

He said, “Truly charity has no limit. For the love of God has been poured into our hearts by His indwelling in each of us, calling us to a life of devotion and inviting us to bloom in the garden where He has planted us and directing us to radiate the beauty and spread the fragrance of His providence.”

Tim, always a wisecracker, said, “You know, I enjoy being in the garden among the blooms, and I do not hear them groaning and struggling to grow.”

Papa laughed and said, “Tim, you get it! God causes the growth. The blooming is a miracle that only God can produce; all we can do is BASK in the light of His love and let His SAP flow. This is how we bloom where we are planted.”

Tim and Esther have learned much from the garden as they lay in their bed. They recall how Papa even used lessons from gardening to prepare them for marriage.

Esther said, “It is wonderful how Jesus uses His creation to demonstrate lessons to help us grow.”

Tim lifted his hands up toward heaven and said, "I bless the Lord with all my soul."

Esther responded by lifting her hands out and said, "Father, I ask you to meet all our needs."

Tim pushed his hands down on the bed and said, "Almighty, I stay right here abiding in you."

And Esther crossed her heart with her arms and said, "Father, I know you love us and will help us grow."

They held each other and fell asleep in the tender mercies of God.

Chew on This: What do images of some of the native flowers, trees, and shrubs do for your human spirit, as you see them in your mind? How does God use nature to inspire us to grow? Can you think of a couple of examples of Jesus using nature to teach a life lesson? What does to mean to BASK, and how does accepting and receiving light cause a plant to grow and bloom (spiritual "photosynthesis")? In nature we marvel at the miracle of a plant growing. How is spiritual growth similar?

How can you BASK in the sunshine of God's love right now? In John, Chapter 15, Jesus speaks of the vine and the branches. Where has God planted you? Are you blooming? What will your life look and feel like when you do? How will this bring God glory? How does God's light and love contribute to your spiritual growth? How do you receive His light and love? Around the fire pit, the group loved to sing:

All creatures of our God and King,

Lift up your voice and with us sing

Alleluia, Alleluia!

Thou burning sun with golden beam,

Thou silver moon with softer gleam,

O praise Him, O praise Him

Thou rushing winds that art so strong,

Ye clouds that sail heaven along,

O praise Him, Alleluia!

Thou rising morn, in praise rejoice,

Ye lights of evening, find your voice,

O praise Him, O praise Him

Alleluia, Alleluia!

Let all things their Creator bless,

And worship Him in humbleness,

O praise Him, Alleluia!

Praise, praise, the Father, praise the Son

And praise the Spirit, Three in One

O praise Him, O praise Him

Alleluia, Alleluia, Alleluia!

Words by St. Francis of Assisi

Born Giovanni di Pietro di Bernadone

Nicknamed “Francesco” by his father

Time, Sunshine, and Devotion

Watching Earl and His horses, Onyx and Ivory, work in the field is a beautiful thing. Tim is proud to be making enough money working with Clay at the blacksmith shop to be able to pay Earl for the work he is doing.

Earl uses hemp rope and hooks that Clay made for him to satchel up the sandstones from the garden plot. The horses are obedient to Earl's commands. Like marching soldiers, they back up into position as Earl talks to them. Then Earl places the hooks, leather straps, and the rope around each stone. Sometimes he has to clear a bit of soil, but when he has a good grip, he gets his team to make the rope taut. Then, on his word, a real bad curse word and a flurry of pirate speak, each horse knows just what to do, and they dig in and pull.

The hamstrings, quads, and calf muscles on these steeds are athletic, and they perform great feats of strength like champions. With their mighty tug, the stones are ejected like popcorn hitting the flame. Then Earl walks them to the gathering place, where he builds little earthen ramps, and masterfully, these horses pull the stones into place, and a good foundation is being erected. When the stone is in place, the horses look proud and enjoy their feed and water. Then Earl walks to the next stone, and the horses follow behind, chomping at the bit to do more work.

These horses love to work. When they dig in and pull, it is with poetic grace. It's truly amazing to see this work being done, and they are a great team. But what you hear is outright savage. Earl is such a calm person by nature, but when that rope is taut, he unleashes a verbal litany of curse words and pirate speak that would make your mom blush.

Yet, Onyx and Ivory each respond like a fighter in a ring. Tim is taken aback by the coarse language that flies off Earl's tongue, but he knows better than to correct him. He has heard Earl say that each horse knows just what to do with each word, and it is impressive. They have a great relationship, and the horses do not act as if they have been degraded.

From Esther, Papa, and Chase, Tim is learning to value relationships and to build them. With Earl, he is being patient and appreciative for the work that is being done.

With Clay, their relationship is blooming like a hibiscus flower with a radiant bloom. Clay is naturally a quiet soul, but his waters run deep. In the shop, Clay is learning to rely on Tim for an extra set of hands and the extra "oomph" that is always needed with heavy metal and wood objects. He is starting to ask Tim questions about life, faith, family, and how he went about building a relationship with Esther. These are meaningful conversations; both men cherish them. It has become abundantly clear to Tim that Clay, who is not only quiet but "earthy," would like a woman in his life, but hasn't a clue as to how to go about it. So, Clay takes a bit of initiative and starts a daily ritual of taking a tea break by going to Breeze's Café and having a pastry and a lime drink, and Tim has his British tea.

While in the café, they dive deeper into some of these conversations about women and relationships. Clay confesses that he is a bit shy. Tim lets him know that he is not just a bit shy, but really shy.

So, these times at Breeze's are a way for Clay to learn how to strike up conversations with the waitresses and have some small talk. Tim thinks he is making great progress and is trying to tell him so. Clay, for being a muscular hulk of a man with hair everywhere, is really a kind and a nice person, who is now open to the idea of having a spiritual and personal relationship with Jesus.

As you can imagine, Tim is careful to encourage him and bring him along, as he knows full well that a relationship with a woman that goes deep into sexual sinning would be a trap. Today, the break has been going really well, and Tim tells Clay that he is going to go out to the dock and just wait awhile, so Clay can have his own conversation with Julie.

Tim is out on the dock and thanking God for all the ways God has been blessing him and Esther. Their work is going well; the land is being cleared; their work relationships are flourishing, and life is good today.

That is until Pug and Brutus recognize Tim and get on each side of him and start pushing him around. You see, there is an unpaid bet between the two of them. While they were on the *Adventurer,* they both knew that this good-looking lad would be propositioned by the strumpets in Port Royal, and that he would lose his virginity quickly. Pug thought it would be the very next day, and Brutus thought it would take a few. They just wanted to find out and pay up.

But, instead of greeting Tim nicely, they force the issue and start a ruckus. This is until Clay heard the commotion and busted out of the café with muscles flexed. When he saw these two pushing Tim around, he didn't ask questions. His left hook to Pug's head was like a hurricane, and his right punch into Brutus's gut was a tornado.

In a flash like lightning, he created a storm, and both Pug and Brutus were thrown into the bay. Clay was not going to let them harm his friend. The scurvy pirates flopped around in the water like drugged fish, because they were either drugged or drunk. They were unable to sail as crew members because of the "crabs" in their britches (sexually transmitted disease). They proved they were not unsinkable. If it were not for some bystanders who pulled them out of the water, they would have drowned.

Clay had to break his conversation with Julie, but Julie was looking at Clay with starry twinkles in her eyes. The area quickly evacuated and turned quiet. Clay hugged Tim's neck and said, "I hope you are all right."

Tim replied, "Those guys were nemeses of mine from the *Adventurer*."

Clay answered, "I didn't like what I saw."

Tim said, "You sure took action!"

They walked past Breeze's Café, and Clay and Tim apologized for the interruption. Clay looked at Julie and asked, "We will talk again? Okay?" Julie just nodded her agreement.

Tim couldn't get over the abrupt explosion of anger that erupted out of Clay to his defense. He just knew that he now had a good friend, but he also knew there was an angry side to Clay that would need to be appeased if he were to have a healthy relationship with a woman. Tim didn't jump into the conversation, but lodged the thought into his mind for a later date.

The next day was extremely overcast, and storm clouds were moving into this side of the island. In the afternoon, the thunder began to crack, and a vicious storm ensued. There must have been the strong winds of a hurricane, or winds the force of a hurricane to go with it. Tim and Esther hunkered down and prayed for calm throughout the night.

The next morning, they took a walk around the garden plot and couldn't believe the big trees that fell, and some were cracked in two. Their first thoughts were of the devastation and how this was a huge setback for them. But, while standing out in the garden, along came Earl with a big smile on his face, with Onyx and Ivory right behind.

Earl said, "I will pull these trees and branches into a pile, and we will have this field cleared in no time. Esther will have some good wood for her oven next year." Earl meant it, and he and his horses dug in to work the field. Tim and Esther couldn't believe the force of the storm and the amount of damage that happened in just a short time. But even more amazing was how quickly the garden repaired. They now had a large pile of wood to watch dry. Earl and his horses came through in a half day of work.

In just a matter of weeks, you couldn't tell that they had been hit by a strong storm. Esther and Papa pointed out to Tim that God was pruning the trees and reshaping them. Tim was awestruck with how nature healed itself so quickly.

In just weeks, the garden was productive and, in some ways, even more beautiful. Tim reckoned life wants to live. The trees and the plants have life in them, and God has given them the ability to regenerate. And then with the produce that had been recently planted in the ground, well, it was in the ground and sprouted up as if it had been kept safe in the ground from the storm. Tim reckoned again at how God's word is like seed and the "seed is in the ground" of our hearts. It was a miracle, Tim observed, in just a short amount of time and with sunshine, this garden regenerated and was whole again and in full bloom.

This stormy experience had resulted in praise. Tim was, once again, amazed with God and wanted to increase his devotion to God. Because of Jesus, he was alive spiritually, and he, too, wanted to live and be even more fruitful. This recovery from the storm with some time and sunshine was another epiphany for Tim. The result of this experience increased in his human spirit the passion to be more devoted to God. But, what does devotion look like and what does it feel like? He just knew he wanted to devote himself more to God as a way of saying thank you to him, for the recovery and renewing work he has done in his life and in the world around him.

This personal revival and spiritual renewal went right along with the recovery and revitalization Tim and Esther were experiencing on their garden plot. Tim made sure to spend time with Papa and talk about this miracle he was witnessing and experiencing. When they had their siesta underneath the shade of a big tree, Papa had the big bill of his Panama hat covering his eyes, as he leaned upon the tree.

But Tim just had to ask, "Papa, how is it that nature can recover so quickly? The flowers are blooming again. The trees are budding, and the seed we planted are germinating and popping out of the ground as if nothing happened."

Papa chuckled and said, "God is good. He has made regeneration possible. He builds it into nature, and that includes us."

Tim asked, "What do you mean us?"

Papa responded, "When you cut yourself, or get scratched, have you ever noticed how, within a few short days, it scabs over and heals?"

Tim said, "Yes, that is good."

Papa replied, "That is not just good. That is a divine design."

Tim leaned in, "What do you mean?"

Papa said, "God doesn't get enough credit for how he has built into the human body the means to recover. It is as if the human body has little workers inside of us that get His orders and go right to work."

Tim rejoiced, "Praise His name!"

Papa shouted, "Amen!"

A big smile rises on Papa's face, and Tim asks, "How does He do it in our garden?"

Papa said, "Look at that beautiful red-billed streamertail hummer working. Amazing, huh? Do you know what it is doing?"

Tim said, "I have heard that it has something to do with pollination."

Papa said, "Very good, Tim. Do you know what that means?"

Tim said, "Not really."

Papa said, "You see these birds flitting around. They dart here and there; they can even flutter backwards."

Tim remarked, "They are amazing."

Papa explained, "They are collecting nectar, getting the magic dust from the male plants. And then they visit female plants and the miracle just blossoms ... do I need to tell you more?"

Tim laughed, "*Land ho*, I get it! And do the bees do the same thing?"

Papa stated, "Yes, and they buzz from flower to flower, and we even get honey from the bees."

Tim said, "Sweet." They both laughed.

Then Tim said, "So, because of the light, together with the rains and the help of the worker bees and hummers, this place is constantly being revived and renewed."

Papa replied, "Yes, now do you see why Francesco talked and sang so much about nature?"

Tim said, "Yes, I do, and Jesus, too."

Papa affirmed and then stated, "So much of what happens in nature we don't see happening, but we see the flower and that maize. The same is with God too: God is invisible. He is Spirit, and we can only worship Him in Spirit and truth."

Tim declared, "I get it. Nature really does reveal the glory of God and teach us much."

Papa exclaimed, "Amen!"

Tim pondered these things in his heart, and wondered out loud with God—practicing His presence—and asked, "Lord, how is the Holy Spirit like a hummingbird and a bee, in my soul? I know you are Light and Love. Cause me to grow, like this garden."

"When the whirlwind passes, the wicked is no more, but the righteous *has* an everlasting foundation" (Proverbs 10:25, NAS).

> "When you pass through the waters, I will be with you; and through the rivers, they will not overflow you. When you walk through the fire, you will not be scorched, nor will the flame burn you" (Isaiah 43:2, NAS).

Chew on This: How is the garden's ability to regenerate an example of the grace of God? How does this truth apply to the "garden" of your mind? What do you think Tim meant when he said "life wants to live?" How is "SAP" (the Spirit and the Anointing) flow related to the Spirit-filled life in the life of a believer in Jesus? What does BASK (Bless, Ask, Stay, Know) have to do with it? The following Scriptures speak of being "made new": 2 Corinthians 5:17; Galatians 6:15; Colossians 3:10. Which one is your favorite? Why? As for Pug and Brutus, why are they not "unsinkable?"

Seed in the Ground

Sid Huston

My life is sound
The seed is in the ground

Planted but, yet, not seen
By faith on Him, I lean

The soil was tilled
The sower's bag was filled

Seed broadcasted far and wide
I stay basking by His side

The seed is planted
Power and life imbued in the seed

With sunshine from above
I bask in His love

Spring showers are refreshing
Pretty flowers will be blooming

The green shoots become robust
Butterflies and bees do something with dust

The seed is in the ground
My life in Him is sound

It takes time for plants to grow
There is much for the gardener to know

Pray, believe, and wait

Fruit cannot be coaxed

Under a blanket of dirt
The seed rests and then the blurt
There is life going on below
In His time, green shoots show

New life begins to sprout
Yet, we fear and fight doubt

We cultivate the ground
And tend to the rows

The fertilizer we throw
Pray, believe, and wait

Only God knows the date
When the green shoots show

We believe and wait
The wind begins to blow

The tender plants lean
As we wait, we water and weed

They germinate
Yet, we wait

Prolifically the green shoots grow
The gardener's face is aglow

So much to forego
When the green shoots show

At season's end, we let it die
The seed pods we spy

In wisdom we let them dry
Life is still inside

When planted they multiply
'Tis true, when born again, we first die

The seasons cycle
There is more shade on the sundial

This is more than survival
Plant life is a miracle

My life is sound
When the seed is in the ground

When the harvest is complete
Ten times, even a hundred and then repeat

There is a time for everything
Under heaven we have cause to sing

My heart is like the ground
His imperishable Word renews my mind

I believe and I am sound
His seed is in the ground

Naturally His fruit shows
His life in me grows

More love He bestows
Opening the pages, His seed sows

The results, He knows
The currents of grace flows

My life is sound
As His seed is in the ground

Pray, believe, wait
The fields are white

The harvest is coming soon
I'll let my roots grow deep

My life is sound
His seed is in the ground.

Hummers, Bees, Taxes, and Freedom

Tim is enamored with the bees that are working in the garden, observing how they collect bitter juices and then miraculously turn them in to sweet honey. This reality has a spellbinding fascination on Tim's fertile mind. He just knows there is a spiritual meaning here, and he is going to capture it before Papa explains it to him.

With Clay, Chase, and Esther, Tim asks, "What else do you know in nature that is bitter, but becomes sweet with God's touch?"

Of all people, Clay was the first to answer, saying, "The lime drink becomes sweet with the sugarcane."

Tim was delighted, and it showed, as he said, "Good thought, Clay."

Clay was encouraged, and Chase added, "That is true with rum, too. If it weren't for the sugarcane, no one would drink the hooch."

They all laughed, and Tim and Esther chided him. Then Esther retold a Bible story, remembering how the children of God were miraculously delivered from slavery in Egypt. And how they escaped the chasing Egyptian army because Moses lifted up his rod, and

God miraculously parted the waters of the Red Sea. The children of God went through the sea, as if they were walking on dry land. Then God pulled the plug, while the Egyptian army was in the middle of it, and they drowned.

Clay and Chase couldn't believe the story and questioned its veracity.

But Esther continued, "One would think that God's children would forever be happy and praise Him, but in hardly any time, they were complaining about food, and, yet, God provided. Then they came to Marah, an oasis, and the water was bitter. But Moses threw the wood in the water, and it was immediately made fresh and sweet."

Tim exclaimed, 'That is amazing! What was in the wood?"

Esther said, "I don't know, but I think it points us to the wood of the cross that Jesus would die on, and how His blood is capable of making bitter hearts pure and sweet, too."

Chase was "Amening," but Clay didn't know what to say. This might have been the first time he heard anything about the cross of Christ.

The garden has recovered quickly. Certainly, Earl and his steeds were a big help. But the honeybees and the hummingbirds seem to be working overtime, and the garden is in glorious full bloom.

Tim thinks, "Is this heaven?"

From the Lord, he receives the thought, "I have been working on heaven for thousands of years, and your garden has taken only a few weeks. Just imagine!" Tim is overwhelmed by what heaven will be like. He thinks no wonder the apostle was given a thorn in the flesh after he had a preview of heaven: It is beyond amazing.

The yellow magic dust from the cone- producing trees and the dust that collects on the bees' wings and on the hummingbirds' tail and chest have fertilized the flowers and crops, and everything seems to be fully alive and healthy. Tim is feeling privileged to be invited by God to join Him in this garden of new creation. That very thought makes Tim think of Clay, because his hope and prayer is for him to become a new creation in Christ. Tim just confidently prays and expects God to do His transforming work in his friend.

Tim is thinking about the pollen and just knows it is full of vitamins, minerals, and the "magic" of some sort of hormone that changes the plants it touches. He is enthralled by the little messengers God uses to do this reproductive work. The streamertail hummingbird is only 4–5 inches large, and the males have a black tail about as long. Only the males have tails, and Tim decides he will not point that out to Esther. They are stunningly beautiful with shimmering green feathers, chest feathers, and a long black tail. That is just the streamertail; yet, the red-billed hummer and the black-billed hummer, and the Jamaican mango hummer have a variety of colors. Jamaicans call the streamertail hummers "doctor birds," and they have iridescent feathers. Tim is captivated by these workers in the garden.

The bees are freaks of nature with little wings, and it doesn't seem possible for them to fly; yet, they can really zip around. They can even hover and fly backwards (so can the hummers). While caught up in the magical and mystical aspect of these amazing workers, Tim experiences an epiphany. Mesmerized by the spiritual thought, inspired by God with nature, Tim wonders out loud, "If I open my life to the Holy Spirit unreservedly, will He pollinate the lives around me? Will these people begin to come alive, blossom, grow, and bear fruit, too?" In prayer, he places Clay, Earl, and Wendolyn and her waitresses before God's throne of grace and, by faith, leaves this request with God.

The next morning Tim and Esther enjoyed their walk and talk as they went to work, reflecting on yesterday's conversation. When Tim met Clay, Clay was in a foul mood. Tim immediately asked what happened.

Clay said, "Tax agents from Britain came by and wanted to collect a large sum of money for the king. (At this time, there were co-monarchs, William and Mary.)

Tim asked, "What do they want to do?"

Clay answered, "They want 15% of everything I fabricate, and 10% of everything I repair.

Tim asked, "How are they going to do that?"

Clay replied, 'They are going to tag and stamp everything that comes off a ship, and they won't let it back on the ship unless it is stamped paid, a tax stamp."

Tim voiced, "How do you feel about that?"

Clay said, "I want to tar and feather 'em."

Tim agreed, "I know. The government knows no bounds. They are the biggest and wealthiest pirates."

Clay growled, "*Arrr.*" Then he continued, "If Governor Morgan were still alive, this would never happen."

Tim asked, "How is that?"

Clay replied, "He appeased the king with Spanish gold."

Tim nodded his understanding. "That is it! Just give the king enough gold, and he will stay off your back."

Clay stated, "I feel as if they have their boot on my throat."

Tim agreed, "*Aye, matey*. They be *jackbooters*."

Tim and Clay got back into their work, and while holding a metal bar red with heat from the fire with tongs, Tim asked, "Why do they need our money anyway? This port is protected by pirates, and it is for pirates. We should take this hot poker and put it where the sun don't shine."

Clay laughed his guts out, as it was so unlike Tim to say such a thing.

Tim responded, "God wants us to be free."

Clay couldn't believe his ears and asked, "I thought religion was about control? You say freedom?"

Tim couldn't hold back his excitement! "Clay, Jesus is all about freedom."

Clay responded, "You mean it?"

With unction, Tim said, "Yes, I do. It was for freedom's sake that Jesus came and died for us."

Clay shaking his head in disbelief asked, "How can that be?"

Tim put down the hot poker in water and it sizzled. Then he said, "Just as God saw the children of Israel in bondage to Egypt's wicked pharaoh and asked Moses to go and set His people free, God sent His son Jesus to set us free, too."

Clay asked, "How did He do it?"

Tim explained, "That is why you see crosses on church steeples."

Clay replied, "I have made one for the church down the street."

Tim declared, "Jesus said, 'You shall know the truth, and the truth will set you free'."

Clay, still unclear, asked again, "But how?"

Tim said, "When we believe Jesus and what He said and did, and trust that He died for our sins and rose again from the dead, we become 'saved,' and now have the ability to be free from sin's control over our lives. We are then free from sin's penalty and sin's power."

Clay asked, “What do you mean?”

Tim smiled and replied, “Sin’s penalty is death, judgment, and hell to pay. Sin’s power is that *scurvy pirate flesh* that wants us to do evil, and be under the control of sin, and sin comes in many forms.”

Clay said, “I will confirm that.”

Tim and Clay had a vigorous day of work and were very productive. Tim couldn’t wait to meet with Esther and tell her of this conversation with Clay and to pray together. The next day Clay was happy to see Tim, and he, for being a quiet man, had a bunch of questions.

Tim was eager to hear them all, and the first out of Clay’s heart was, “Tim, if God wants us free, does that apply to the government, too?”

Tim listened very well. He thought awhile, and then he spoke, “Clay, I believe so. The reasons governments are so heavy-handed is because we do not love and trust each other. Nor do we serve naturally with gladness and with selfless giving. So, the government becomes the power and the authority. Usually, it’s an autocrat, an aristocracy (many wealthy families), or an oppressive regime, like a dictator with his thugs.”

Clay responded, “I get it. Governor Morgan set up shop and ran a law-and-order place even though it was a very wicked and corrupt place.”

Tim remarked, “But, imagine if people were subject to God and lived like Jesus. I mean they loved sacrificially, lived honestly, and really loved God and the people in their community. Don't you think we could experience freedom?"

Clay said, "I think we could."

Tim said, "It would be like heaven on earth, huh!"

Clay answered, "It sounds beautiful, but too good to be true."

Tim replied, "I think it is as simple as living the Golden Rule."

Clay chuckled, "Is that, he who has the gold rules?"

Tim laughed and then explained, "The Golden Rule is, 'Do unto others as you would like them to do unto you'."

Clay admitted he had heard that before. Tim suggested, "But why not give it a try? If we live in the Spirit, walk in the light of God's love, BASK in His presence, and live honest and truthful lives, I think God will help us have communities and even countries of 'freemen and women'." Clay was speechless, but Tim observed him nodding his agreement. Maybe it was a glimmer of hope.

When they took their break at Breeze's Café, they continued their conversation. Tim said, "I have been thinking about these beautiful hummingbirds, looking at one working a flower by the café. They are free and productive. I don't see anyone taxing them."

Clay laughed and said, "But they sure are beautiful, free, and they do work hard."

Tim agreed, and over a glass of lime drink sweetened with plenty of sugarcane, they enjoyed the conversation. Tim mused, "I believe God shows us what life can be like in nature. I believe if we trust God and ask Him to forgive our sins and to become who He is in us, He is the Lord of our lives. We become people who love, trust, and regard others as important. We live the CARE principle that Papa always talks about."

Clay commented, "I get it. I like what I am hearing."

Chew on This: What spiritual lessons do you think Tim captured from looking at the different ways hummingbirds and bees work? What did you learn in this illustration? According to Exodus 15:25, the waters of Marah became fresh and sweet from the wood that Moses threw in. What is your insight here? Could this be a foreshadowing of the cross where Jesus died (see 1 Peter 2:24 for more insight)? Why do you think Tim was being patient with Clay and didn't force him to make a decision for Christ?

Why do governments tend to be overbearing with laws, taxes, regulations, and agents? What did the founders of America hope for when America created a Constitution, The Bill of Rights, and our Declaration of Independence?

We truly have something special in our United States. What are our federal government's responsibilities? What are your individual rights and responsibilities? Do you think God wants us to be free (John 8:32–36) and to be free from sin's control and domination (Romans 8:1–11)? Do you think God wants the USA to remain as the “land of the free and the home of the brave?” If so, what needs to happen?

God's Beautiful Garden of Grace

Life is good for this little Christian community that is being built behind Port Royal, Jamaica. These folks are loving God, enjoying nature, and loving and serving one another. Their little group is growing. People are being added, and everyone is encouraged to see the spiritual growth. Papa is doing a Bible series on the kinds of grace God has for believers in Jesus. Clay has started to attend and is actively listening, but some wonder if he is coming just because Julie has started to attend per Esther's invitation. The group isn't being judgmental. They just know God is at work all around them.

Today Tim and Esther once again enjoyed the "rut of routine" and walked to Lime Street in the cool of the morning. They had a pleasant conversation and loved being able to share in each other's day. They imparted a blessing to each other with a kiss. Then each went to their work. Tim was now looking forward to having a break during each shift and checking in with Esther as Clay really liked visiting Breeze's Café. He also liked seeing Julie, and Tim liked a few minutes with Esther, too. Life is good today!

However, when Tim walked into the blacksmith shop, he heard deep and painful groaning in the back of the shop. He scampered around and discovered that Clay was bound up by hemp rope and gagged. Clay was very fortunate he didn't gag and die on his vomit. Tim quickly untied him, and Clay was in a ton of pain. He had a big lump on his head, and, as far as he could tell, his right arm was broken. Tim got him some water to drink and to rinse out his mouth. Then Clay began to recount the events of late last night.

Tim wanted to know if it were the tax agents from the British government. Clay knew it was the pirates who brought in a brace for a mast to be repaired. He said they just ganged up on him and beat the crap out of him. He could make out who they were by the flicker of the flame he keeps lit in the pit. He thought for sure they were going to kill him, but they hit him with a club to his head and shoved him up to the anvil. He just knows his arm is broken. It hurts badly, and he can barely move it.

Putting first things first, Tim tended to Clay and made a sling for his ailing right arm. Then he got some tree bark for Clay to chew on as a pain reliever. Then Clay suggested that Tim go to the dock and see if the pirate ship had left the port. Sure enough, with just a glance, Tim could see that a ship was leaving, and it was missing a mast pole and missing a sail. He just knew these pirates would get out at sea and *splice their brace*. Tim took the observation back to Clay, and they discussed the costs and disadvantages of working with and for pirates. He thought for certain they wanted to kill him as "dead men tell no tales." Then he said, "I hope their ship leaks like a sieve, and they choke on the *bilge* water."

Tim laughed and said, "God has a way of making things right. Vengeance belongs to Him."

Clay grunted in pain, "*Aye.*"

Tim said, "I am just glad that I am not on that ship. Bad company corrupts good morals."

Clay said, "*Sí, sí.* I'd feed them all to the fish. They are bottom feeders and worthless *freebooters.*"

They both had a good laugh and decided to go to Breeze's Café and talk about how they were going to go about their business with Clay in this condition. At the café, the ladies were accommodating, as one of them got a towel and began to clean up Clay's wounds, and Julie was there to comfort him. Clay enjoyed the attention, and his pain wasn't so bad with all of the tender loving care and consolation he was receiving.

The men talked about their work orders and decided that they would try to fulfill them while Clay's arm was in the sling, by Tim doing the heavy lifting and Clay giving the instruction. They both knew they wouldn't be able to do as much, as it was going to take a while for Clay's arm to mend and gain strength. Tim was willing to be Clay's "right-hand" man. Clay mentioned that more time at Breeze's Café was in the plan.

During their conversation, Clay mentioned that he really did like Papa's teaching and thought that they should take some time to talk about the lessons together. Clay even mentioned, "This bit of down time might be good for me." Tim nodded his encouragement and was happy to know that the Word of God was having a positive impact on his friend.

At the Bible study, Papa said, "I have been thinking about the garden. Do you know about the Garden of Eden? But, also, here we have a garden, and it has recovered quickly from the big storm. Its glory has returned, and I am inspired to talk with you about God's beautiful and bountiful garden of grace. This will take several lessons, as I want us to learn all we can about God's marvelous grace."

The group was encouraged and Papa "waxed" on about how the garden is an example of God's grace. He explained that, even though we have work to do in the garden, the garden is an example of grace. The gardenlike grace is a gift not deserved. God provided the soil and the climate—even the sunshine. He even created the seeds and made so many unique plants that are beautiful that provide us with fruit, vegetables, wood, and nuts. And of course, many magnificent flowers thrill our souls. In the same way, God has provided us with a beautiful garden of grace in His holy Word. He has given us a colorful and beautiful bouquet of grace.

As Papa looked out upon his students, some of their eyes were filled with wonder, but some looked confused.

So, he explained, "God loves us unconditionally. We can't work and earn His love, and we don't deserve it because of our attempts to live a righteous life. If you believe you are a Christian because of something you have done to gain some standard of righteousness, and appease God, then you do not understand grace. We have all sinned. We are all like filthy pirates, and we deserve hell. And worse, there is nothing we can do about it. But God is a God of grace and loves us, anyway, and provides a way to take our sin problem out of the way: by having our sins nailed on that cross with Jesus. He then shed His blood.

"If we believe, He forgives all our sin and washes us clean. We now can come before Him, enjoy Him, and go to heaven when we die, because God, being holy, will not allow sin, or a sinful person, into His presence. What makes heaven so glorious is not just the beauty of the heavenly garden, but the absence of sin. By His grace He makes us completely righteous, so we can enjoy His presence. This is why we will be right at home in heaven. And, this is the reason heaven will be so beautiful."

The group was encouraged, and they were hanging on his every word. Then Papa responded, "For by grace we are saved. Not as a result of our works. None of us can boast about what we have done. God has done it all. Salvation is not deserved by any of us. Salvation is by His grace alone. And by faith alone."

Everyone was nodding their agreement and had a look of gratitude on their faces. Papa continued, "Grace is God's favor: His acceptance of us and embracing us with His love. Jesus died for all our sins and He died for everyone. It is even by His grace that we can choose to believe. He helps us to believe and to walk by faith. But before we look at God's beautiful garden of grace, we must realize that we are like pirates, and we have *scurvy pirate flesh.* We have broken God's commandments and moral laws. We are doomed to die, and being dead in our trespasses and sins. Judgment Day will come, and there will be hell to pay. Sinners will go to eternal torment in hell: in the outer darkness where there is weeping, screaming, and gnashing of teeth. Hell is a terrible place and a high price to pay for sinning. But if you truly believe in Jesus, you have a new nature and a completely new identity as a righteous child. You are now considered a holy saint. Therefore, you belong with Him in His heaven. This is what I mean by 'wearing the CROWN'."

Even Tim and Esther were taken aback by the harsh description about judgment coming from Papa. Then Papa declared, "What I am saying is the truth. We need to digest the bad news before we can truly appreciate the good news. And the good news is that, while we were yet sinners, Jesus died for us. This is grace. God has a whole beautiful garden of His grace to give us."

Clay leaned into Tim and said, "I want to believe all of this, but to see myself as a saint?"

There was a holy hush coming over the group. Everyone was quiet, and then Papa continued, "The first 'grace' I want to talk with you about is called 'common grace.' As you know, God causes it to rain on the righteous and the unrighteous. God loves everyone, and this message of His love and acceptance is meant to go out to the whole world."

Tim asked, "Even pirates?" Clay let out an "*arrr.*"

Papa said, "Yes, even pirates. We are all pirates that are born again by His Spirit."

The group continued to be encouraged, and Papa went on, "We can walk out into our garden and pick an orange, a lime, nuts, or an avocado from a tree. Think about it: We didn't plant that tree, water it or tend it, but God, by His grace, gives us so much fruit from these trees. This is an example of common grace. And this grace is for everyone. We can bask in the sunshine, enjoy the breezes, smell the roses, and taste the honey from the honey bee."

Chase yelled out, "Taste the roasted meat from the cow!"

Frieda squawked in glee and said, "Cow, cow, cow."

Nick, while laughing, exclaimed, "We don't have to be religious!"

Papa cheered and declared, "Nick, that is good! It is not by some religious good works or rituals where we earn this common grace; this grace currents out of God's nature. God is love."

This was a meaningful time for the group, because they were starting to get the message about grace. The people were understanding how God so loved this world and has given us so much, to demonstrate His love. Papa went on to talk about water, air, sunshine, and refreshing breezes, implying, if it weren't for the grace of God, life here on earth would be unbearable.

He said, "We just need to practice God's presence and learn to bask in the sunshine of His love."

He then continued, "Some of you are new to faith in Jesus, but did you know that there is a 'preparing' grace that God put around you so that you would come to Him?"

Clay was taking this to heart. He bowed his head into his chest.

Papa said, "When a person comes to faith, they can look back and see how God was orchestrating things, events, people, and experiences to help them get out of their self and open their hearts to Him."

The group was doing some "amening," and Papa said, "In God's garden of grace, our hearts are like pretty flowers opened up to His light like a flower opening to the sun above."

The group had been thrilled by this practical teaching, and they enjoyed some mango pie Esther and Julie brought. The fellowship was sweet, too, because people were impressed with the grace of God.

Tim mentioned to Clay, as he was savoring a sweet bite of Esther's mango pie, "This pie is all about grace. We didn't plant or pick the mango, or process the sugar or make the crust. We get to enjoy it. This is grace."

Clay rolled his eyes. Tim, with a big smile stated, "Grace is mango pie." Clay rolled his eyes again and smiled his understanding.

The next day, Clay had lots to say. For a quiet man, it was a lot. When Tim showed up at the shop, Clay was feeling good. His arm wasn't hurting anymore, and he was stretching it out and exercising, by using pieces of wood and curling them like a weightlifter. Now he could use it a bit, and he felt like he was making a comeback. But, most important to him was the talk about grace. He asked, "Did Papa really mean it, that even a pirate could get saved and go to heaven?"

Tim assured Clay, "Yes, Jesus died for sinners. Anyone who believes can be forgiven and free." Clay thought about this, and they went to work trying to straighten out the barrel of a gun.

They had a good day working in the shop. Clay just seemed to be at peace about things. Tim reckoned that Clay was seeing the invisible hand of God leading him to Himself, and Tim was at peace, too.

In the following months, Clay didn't miss a meeting. Yet, because he couldn't read, he would listen and then ask Tim to explain things in the shop the next day. Tim felt fulfilled to be able to help a friend grow in faith.

It took several months of study for Papa to touch on aspects of grace. It was a "blooming" time of study for everyone, and they just loved these lessons on the "garden of God's grace." Everyone was built up and encouraged by these teachings. Truly, they were growing in the grace and knowledge of Jesus.

Clay had a difficult time trying to understand "sanctifying" grace. But Tim used a bent metal rod to explain. He told Clay that sanctification is the process where God takes our behaviors and straightens them out and aligns them to our true identity.

He explained, "This crooked rod was once straight, and now with some heat, we can make it straight again. Tim also said, "Not everyone who believes in Jesus allows Jesus to conform their attitudes and behaviors to Him." Clay understood what he was saying.

In this study, Papa taught on "saving grace," "sanctifying grace," "staying and sustaining grace," "wisdom grace," "fear of the Lord grace," "provisional grace," "enabling and empowering grace," "serving grace," and "dying grace." Tim had a big and wonderful time helping Clay apply these lessons to his life. All in all, Tim and Clay came to see the sufficiency of God's grace. Whenever they had a struggle, they would laugh and ask, "God, do you have a grace for this?" For sure, Tim had a fresh and new understanding about the beautiful garden of grace he got to work in.

Chew on This: According to Romans 8:28, how did Clay's injuries work out for his good? What do you think it means to "grow in grace?" How does a person do this? Why must we understand the "bad news" to appreciate the "good news?" According to Romans 3:23 and 6:23, what is the cost of our sinning? What is the free gift of God? Why is this called grace? How do you define grace? Why can't grace be earned or deserved? Why then is the gospel called good news? (See Ephesians 2:8–10.)

Grace for When Your World Sinks

Family means everything to Tim, Esther, and Papa, but, to their delight, their little church community has really taken on a family feeling. The people are happy to have added Wyndolyn, Clay, Julie, and now Christina is joining in, too. She works at the Black Dog Saloon, just a couple of establishments down from Breeze's.

A real and sincere fellowship of encouragement is endearing to all. The other day, they, the church group, were down by the bay, and Papa was baptizing some of them. Unbeknown to the group, shy Clay was not only baptized, but he sang a song about the cross, a song that he had heard Esther sing. This was a blessed time for their entire group. Clay has a nice voice, a deep baritone, and has added depth to the group's hymn singing times. The joy bells are ringing in Port Royal.

Clay let the group know how much the group meant to him, and that he was happy to have come to faith in Jesus. He also mentioned his arm was almost healed and explained how Tim had told him the story of Samson in the Bible. He said he could relate to him and mentioned, as Samson's hair grew back out, his strength was renewed. He said he, too, was feeling strong again. The group cheered his progress both spiritually and physically.

This feeling of family has spilled over, and now Tim and Esther are hoping to have a baby. They both wonder why she is not yet pregnant, but they are enjoying the process and are keeping this prayer request before God. A wonderful sense of belonging has made even Earl feel better about himself. From time to time, he, too, comes for a service or a study. He is also very proud to have worked on the gathering place. The group is appreciative of his work with Onyx and Ivory, as he has finished building the walls out of irregular stones. The roof has been put on, so the group now has a meeting place on the hill overlooking the garden.

The roof was framed with local timber, and palm fronds provide the cover, and they work remarkably well. Papa didn't let the history of palm fronds go without mention. He said, "In the Mediterranean world, the palm frond was sacred to most religions, as they were a symbol of victory, triumph, peace, and even eternal life."

So when the members of this community looked up at the roof, this is what they were thinking about. Papa talked at great length at how they were used in Jesus' triumphal entry into Jerusalem. This little community loves having their own place, and Tim and Esther do not mind that one half of it is their home.

The next day, just before quitting time, Clay told Tim to quit a bit early. With his arm working again, he could finish the project by himself. Tim left the shop early, so he could have some time at Breeze's Café and be there to walk Esther home.

It was unfortunate that they broke from their routine, because, no sooner had Tim left, than three intruders invaded the premises. Clay remembered this motley crew from his past. Bildad, Sophar, and Eljaz were men that Clay used to carouse with. Men who were bored because their pirate ship had sunk. Clay knew immediately that they were up to no good. Probably looking to steal something to support whatever bad habits they had, or just to eat.

At first, he thought they might want to talk about old times, but Bildad mentioned that they had witnessed his baptism from the dock, and now they thought he was too good for them. Clay told them that wasn't the truth, and before he could talk about his life's new direction, Sophar was swinging a heavy chain that he and Tim had fashioned.

They told Clay he was going to get the "third baptism." But as Sophar was winding up for a swing with the chain, it was too heavy for him. Clay reached and grabbed it out of his hand and swung it back at him, missing him completely, but landing a blow on Eljaz's head. Sophar and Bildad knew instantly that they were in deep trouble and ran for the dock.

Eljaz was lifelessly curled up in a heap on the dirt floor. Dead as a doornail. Clay fell to his knees and prayed for Eljaz's soul and wept for his own loss, because he didn't want to hurt anyone, let alone kill Eljaz. His next first thought was, "Is there grace for this?"

Tim and Esther just happened to see Sophar and Bildad running away from the shop and knew something was wrong. Tim assumed that they had seen, from the dock, Tim leave the shop early and moved in on an opportunity for theft.

Tim sprinted to the shop, and Esther moved at a lady's pace. Upon entering the shop, he heard a sound he had never heard before: Clay was sobbing. When Tim saw the dead man on the floor, he knew what had happened. He knew that the scoundrels had tested Clay and met their match. After hugging Clay and consoling him, he understood this was an accident. Tim let Clay know that God's grace was sufficient for this and wouldn't withhold any love from him or hold him in judgment. Clay responded as if he understood, too, but insisted that they needed to go to Parrot's Place, as he needed to speak his peace. Esther didn't want Tim to go along, but Tim had the resolve to support his friend and they went. Esther followed at a distance and remained on the boardwalk.

Upon entering Parrot's Place, there was a raucous commotion going on, but as soon as Clay made his presence known, the place became eerily quiet. Peering through the crowd, Clay could see Sophar and Bildad shrinking down in the back of the room. Looking right at them Clay conveyed, "Your friend Eljaz is dead. And I killed him by accident. I meant to hurt you two, because you threatened to harm me. I am sorry; we will give him a respectful burial."

Then Clay and Tim walked out with godly sorrow on their faces. Esther was there and asked, "Why did you need to go to Parrot's Place?"

Clay explained, "I needed to clear the air and my conscience." The next day Clay and Tim contacted Earl and commissioned him and his horses to dig a grave for Eljaz. Papa Peter helped with a graveside service that was God-honoring and attended by this small family of believers. Clay and Tim made a cross out of metal and wood rail from the pile in the shop as a marker. Clay paid for Earl's services out of his own bag of loot.

For the next few months, wherever Clay went around the port, there was a hush. People were quiet around him, and he knew everyone was talking. They were sure not to bother him, but Clay really wasn't bothered, as he knew in his heart that God, the righteous Judge, knew what had transpired and loved him regardless.

But, with God's people, there was only affirmation and encouragement. Papa continued to teach on the marvelous grace of God, and every lesson comforted Clay and the group. He was happy to have identified with Christ in baptism and being called a killer was no different than being called a sinner. Now Clay knew he was a righteous man and that there was fresh water running under his bridge. The cross where Jesus died had become his bridge over troubled water.

Clay felt whole and God's grace was a healing balm to his soul. The death of Eljaz was a good reminder to Tim and Clay that life is short, and they just enjoyed taking longer breaks at Breeze's Café and talking about the things in life that we value as most important. On this day, Clay and Tim were at Breeze's, when they saw Dr. Reverend Emmanuel Heath on the boards outside, and they cordially greeted each other. The good reverend mentioned that he just had prayers at St. Paul's Anglican Church and was to meet his friend John White on the dock. Tim and Clay observed these friends meeting up.

As history will tell it, they went to a nearby tavern, and a couple of goblets of wormwood wine were served and downed. Then Mr. White lit his pipe and leaned back in his chair. The floor began to shake, and before White could shout, "Lord, Sir, what is this?" the Reverend Heath had pulled his cassock up around his waist and started sprinting past Breeze's Café. Tim, Esther, Clay, Julie, Wendolyn, and others followed with haste. Sprinting up the shale hill, they looked back, only to see Port Royal being rolled into the deepwater bay. In just a few moments of horror, a good portion of the 53 acres that made up the bay area were sunk into the water with a loud clap.

The sandy areas just dropped off, and the sand looked like waves, as the floor of this world was dropped into the sea. It was as if God was shaking out a rug, and people were tossed and devoured by the abyss. They heard screams, and, yet, there were just the sounds of lumber cracking and bricks banging. Everything was splashing and the sea gurgling. There was nothing these good people could do but watch the destruction and devastation happen; it was all so abrupt. They kept their distance, and, in just minutes, there was a tidal wave, a tsunami of water tossing bodies out of the sea. Even a ship was lifted over the rooftops, onto the street that was once behind the bay. They could read that it was the HMS *Swann*. It was tossed up on the buildings like a little boy throwing a toy.

Three earthquakes cracked, and, nearby, a mountain was cut in half, like a baker slicing a cake and pushing it off the plate into the trash. The entire community below it on the more level ground was covered by massive tons of earth. Limestone and clay made it a natural grave, as the material tumbled all the way out to the bay.

In the streets behind what were the shops on Port Royal Bay, bodies were floating lifeless in the street. There were more than 2,000 immediate deaths from these unnatural actions. Ships were capsized, and, instantly, buildings made of wood and brick vanished, as if someone had pulled the rope to a trap door. Worst of all, the people on the insides were swallowed up by the crevices made in sea and sand. The earth just seemed to open up, and the sea flushed them down. This band of believers on the rock-hewn bank looked at each other wide-eyed and, yet, at peace. They were being infused with grace for this; yet, it was surreal.

In just minutes, Earl was there with his steeds. He had with him a long hemp rope, and the few people who were alive and bobbing in the water were pulled out. One of the survivors was Christina, as the backwash had pulled her out into the bay. The group was happy to save her, and the women embraced her in love. Earl just went about his business, and the horses were champions, obeying his every command, as spicy as those commands were.

The group waited till the rumbling stopped, but immediately stepped into rescue mode. Washed up on the new bank, that was once the interior of Port Royal, were the dead bodies of Sophar and Bildad. Ironically, they were found outside the rock jail house that had been ripped in two. Tim could only wonder what happened to Pug and Brutus. They were mean to Tim. Did God make them "*feed the fish*?"

Chase and Nick were doing their part to rescue and save whoever was still alive. Some people were held captive to the earth, stuck in the mud; yet, out in the water, Earl threw the rope to them, hoping to pull them to safety. He knew full well that when the tide rose or another wall of water crashed down, they would drown. There was the look of inevitability on their faces, as they all wanted to live. "Life wants to live" is a law of nature, they thought. Nick found a pocket watch in the hand of a drowned soul, and the time read 11:43. The date was June 7, 1692.

The group refused to be discouraged. There were pirate types going from house to house and looting everything of value. Instead of rescuing the perishing and lending a hand to helping people live and recover, they were doing what pirates do. They were raiding and pillaging, filling their own treasure chest with valuable loot. *Scurvy pirate flesh* sees the misfortune of one as an opportunity for self. These looters were so weighted down with stolen goods that the group wondered what they could do with it. Yet, in the days that followed, they pawned it off, in Kingston, as they found a boat and toted it there.

The selfishness of man knows no limits. The remnant ideology of Captain Morgan resonated even through this tragedy. But, for this band of Christian people, the things of eternity took on a greater value. God's promises, God Himself, and a person's spirit and soul were of more value than the trinkets the pirates were taking.

Proving that *scurvy pirate flesh* has no limits, people were looting, drinking, smoking, and whoring by the end of this very long day. Some pirates were fleecing the pockets of the washed-up dead and claiming chains and loot for themselves. They would lop off fingers to capture gold rings. Such is the way of the pirate. God noticed the hearts of these evil people, too. He didn't look away.

Amazingly, the group was able to work the rest of the day with a boost from adrenaline, but motivated out of reverent fear. Tim and Esther wondered if they would be able to sleep because of the loss, struggle, and horror. Yet, there was grace for them, and God gave them sleep. Goodness and mercy followed them home, and they had peace.

Chew on This: On June 7 at 11:43, Port Royal collapsed into the deepwater bay. Prior to the earthquakes, Tim and Clay were spending more time at Breeze's Café just talking about life. How did this prepare them for the destruction? How do you think God used this experience to bond the Christian group together?

How is it that pirate-types could continue stealing after witnessing such destruction? What does it tell you about the condition of man? (Look up Jeremiah 17:9 and jot down your thoughts.) Pirates do what pirates do. Behavior currents out of how they see and believe themselves to be. How was this also true of Tim, Esther, and the Christian community, as well?

The Pocket Watch

Sid Huston

It was a stopped pocket watch
Found in Port Royal Harbor

This was in 1692
The time on its face was 11:43 in the a.m.

It was at this exact time of the day
Port Royal City sank in the bay

An earthquake shook the area
In no time a couple thousand more would die of malaria

Yet, instantly hundreds were squashed or drowned
A storehouse for the West Indies was this little town

It was also the world's most wicked city
Captain Henry Morgan made it morally filthy

He knew what sailing men would like to get
When they bolted off their dirty ship

Rum, whores, and pig on a spit
Eat, sleep, and time to sit

Morgan was a ruthless and mean man
He feasted on the riches of the Spanish Main

He had lucrative hauls from Cuba,
Portobelo, Panama, and Venezuela
He would strip them of their wealth

Squeeze them with rope, and they
would yell where it was held

Then he would *yo-ho-ho* and be off with the horde
Doesn't this wanton greed strike a chord?

He made Port Royal into a pirate haven
To be clear, it was nothing like heaven

He deserved to be gibbeted
His bowels should have been exhibited

At home in England, they did swoon
They were delighting in his chest of *doubloons*

With pockets filled with *pieces of eight*
People tend to forget about their final date

They forget about God
Because of the attractions on this dirt clod

People fill their time with all that is sensual
And forget about all that is consequential

So, it was with Port Royal, Jamaica,
When it comes to the spiritual, you
just can't really fake it

Pompeii and Sodom and Gomorrah
Also labeled as the most wicked places on Earth

They, too, had a spiritual dearth
Archeologists would take centuries to unearth
The time was 11:43 in the morning
The earth started rumbling, imagine the screaming?

God is not ever really mocked
Concerning time, He is not docked

It is up to us to get in His rhyme
We all know that we have committed crime

For no one but God knows the time
When His pocket watch will chime

Judgment Cliff (Lex Talionis)

Papa Peter met with the group before they joined Earl with his steeds and a large wagon. He said, "Tertullian, a church father of old said, 'The blood of the martyrs is the seed of the church,' but I believe the death of pirate sinners is fertilizer and the impetus for us to live a righteous life. God wants us to grow into beautiful trees that bring healing to those who remain. As we work today, let's think about the righteousness of God and His grace that keeps on saving us. Remember, He saves us forevermore."

There was so much work to do. It had to be done quickly before the dead bodies bloated and became maggot-infested. This team knew what they had to do, and they were determined to get after it. There was grace and strength for this. They worked well together, though they had a ton of questions about what happened and if God was mad and judging everyone.

The devastation in Port Royal was the result of both geologic and spiritual conditions. The port was built on sandy ground, as unwise people will do. Liquefaction occurred, and the place was poised to slide into the sea. When the earthquakes happened, a landslide occurred in the ground and underwater in the sea shelf. But it is obvious that this was a judgment action from God. The people were decadent, debauched, sexual sinners, perverted, thieving, disobedient to God's laws, and naturally vile, crude and debased, slave traders, and spiritually apathetic without thought or concern for God. This place was a pirate haven developed by Captain Henry Morgan, who was a symbol of pirate greed. It is apparent that God had been patient, but like in the days of Noah, He had had enough.

"The Lord is watching everywhere, keeping His eye on the evil and the good" (Proverbs 15:3, NLT).

Therefore, God, because of His holy character, had to act. People forget that He is the Judge and is actively confronting sin and sinners. But more, Papa Peter reminded everyone that God is "holy, holy, holy." When he observed the destruction, he said, "Holy cow" (unholy cow)! Remember, this place was started by buccaneers, who were cattle thieves.

Gratefully, God judged sin once and for all time on the cross when Jesus died, but often people forget this truth, many have not heard this truth, or simply neglect this truth. In Jesus' teaching about the wheat and the tares, the wheat and the weeds would get uprooted together. Sadly, today the group of Christians who are cleaning up the aftermath of this destruction will discover some friends who they think are "wheat," yet, got uprooted with the weeds that were destined for destruction.

This knowledge makes it even more grievous to work; yet, they "tend to the garden." Some good people they knew were found face down in the flooded streets. This was tough to take, because the Word declares that "When the storms of life come, the wicked are whirled away, but the godly have a lasting foundation" (Proverbs 10:25, NLT).

Even though there were lots of questions in each one's mind about God's judgment here, they would store them up and sort out their thoughts later, because for now there was work to do. Earl was busy with Onyx and Ivory digging some big graves not far from the garden, and soon he would hitch up the big wagon and bury the dead there. The horses seemed to be up for this huge task.

The streets were filled with stinking corpses, and soon bugs and rats would be feasting on these carcasses. Tim couldn't help but think, "Vengeance is mine; I will repay, saith the Lord" (Romans 12:19, KJV).

As always, Chase was there for a bit of perspective saying, "God always has the last word. *Arrr*!"

Nick and Clay remained silent; they just knew this was a day they would never forget. How they had the strength to lift these heavy, lifeless bodies into the wagon was a testament to their human strength and to God's gifting them with muscles and energy.

Papa couldn't help but philosophize as he, too, pitched in to help. He just knew the legacy of Port Royal would be compared to Pompeii and Sodom, the two other cities that were called "the wickedest cities in the world," and they are no, no, no more, gone for good, snuffed out. The history of a pirate-led and a kept port for pirates had run its course and came to its inevitable end. The pirate greed, promiscuity, and wanton merriment was over. This is the result of people thinking that God wasn't paying attention. Disregard for God's holy nature and His grace and mercy brought about this catastrophic result.

Papa, Tim, Esther, and, in fact, the whole group didn't understand why the righteous folks had to do the clean-up work and risk their lives, but they also knew that they were the ones left to tend the garden. And they knew they had to work with dispatch, as the corpses would soon be bloating, stinking, and maggot- infested if they were not buried soon. For certain, if they didn't work fast, it was only going to get worse.

They reckoned that God arose and purged Port Royal of her filth. He judged the people, and good people who remained had to answer the call. It is also good to think about sin and its consequences. Perhaps some people would wise up while they were still alive and being attended to. Ironically the HMS *Swann*, the ship that was washed up on top of houses and buildings, was now being used as a sanctuary to care for people.

Looking at the ship, Papa thought of a "black swan" event and thought this out-of-place ship fit the description. This devastation was as weird as a black swan. For it, too, was difficult to predict, highly impactful, difficult to understand, difficult to prepare for, and, yet, looking back, it was inevitable. Surely these severe consequences and widespread damage occurred because these people deserved the spanking of God's judgment. And if not for a repentant heart, it will happen again.

It is rare to see a black swan, but we must pay attention is what Papa was thinking. He knew his band of growing Christians must not just move on. They needed to think, to grieve, and gain the resolve to live a righteous and holy life consistent with their true identity in Christ. He reckoned God was at work all around them, and He is paying attention, so they (and we) must pay attention to Him in everything. Certainly, God had spoken, is speaking, and they just knew He wasn't silent.

Esther was feverishly doing her part, preparing food and getting the gathering place ready to receive the infirm. By the end of the day, another 800 people would die in the aftermath of the earthquakes: the tsunami and the backwash. Now people were going to die of starvation, dysentery, malaria, influenza, and other diseases. The group remained resilient and were confident in the immune systems the good Lord had given them. They just did their work, in the power of the Holy Spirit, and left the results to God.

Word had gotten back to the group that 60 kilometers away, the once proud mountain that stood so tall would now be called "Judgment Cliff." The people couldn't believe how stark it looked. A man from the community below it, who was already chasing after a runaway bull, found himself running for his life when the tremors quickened his spirit. Still filled with adrenaline, he said, "A great mountain split and fell into the level land covering several settlements." More than a couple of plantations were covered with clay, shale, and lava rock. More than 20 people he knew of were buried deep under the half of the mountain that fell on them.

Now what remained was a sheer and stark cliff, jutting straight up with a bold face. The man said, "If that cliff face could speak, it would say, 'Leave, and don't mess with God'." In just days, the cliff had a new name, Judgment Cliff. He went on to say no one wants to get close ... just the sight of the cliff causes hearts to tremble. He said, "God has poured out His indignation. His anger against us for our sinning burned hot."

The man was invited to the gathering place and was comforted with fresh baked bread and jam from Esther. He was extremely grateful, but he couldn't stop talking. Certainly, he was a man of faith and knew God had miraculously saved him. He said, "I have heard that there is a reward for the righteous; surely God judges this Earth." Everyone got the idea that this man escaped by providence and by the skin of his teeth. Perhaps that was no mere bull, maybe an angel?

This man believed that there was no escape except for the grace of God. His heart was still pumping with adrenaline. He had traveled nearly 60 kilometers on foot since the mountain fell.

The group was grateful to celebrate this man's salvation and to welcome him into their fellowship. They all enjoyed fresh food away from the stench of the flooded streets of Port Royal. As a group, they could scarcely believe how God had given them the energy and grace to contend with the gruesome work they did today. They were grateful and pleased to put this day to bed. It would be difficult to sleep because their minds were wrestling with uncomfortable and deep theological thoughts.

There were still corpses to contend with tomorrow. They knew that God rained on Sodom and Gomorrah with fire and brimstone from heaven and let Mount Vesuvius entomb wicked Pompeii with hot lava. They had just witnessed God cutting their city off the earth with earthquakes. What they heard about Judgment Cliff was a reminder to them that on Mount Golgotha—also known as Mount Calvary—another stark cliff, God had judged all their sins on the cross where Jesus died by shedding His blood for their forgiveness of sins. Knowing this was firm in their heads, but in truth, they were all trembling in reverent fear.

The next morning, Papa told them about *Lex Talionis,* stating that most people in the world know that there is a law of judgment written on our hearts. He was sure the *scurvy pirate* people of Port Royal had become so calloused that they had no feeling or understanding of this "law."

He knew what his flock needed most. They needed to be comforted by God's love and affirmed by His truth. They also needed the assurance that comes from His promises. Papa reminded them that "The storms of life come; the wicked are whirled away, but the godly have a lasting foundation." Papa assured the group that comfort would come, not to live by their feelings, but to trust God and to live by faith in Him and His promiscs. He told them to rely on Him and to believe truth, stating they were secure in His love.

Chew on This: Do you believe the death of pirate sinners can be the impetus for believers in Jesus to live a righteous life? If so, why? What is it about the holiness and righteousness of God that motivated Him to destroy Port Royal? What did this act produce? Do you believe God watches you and will judge your sin? Didn't He already have Jesus pay the penalty for all your sin on the cross?

There are lots of Scriptures on the judgments of God: Romans 14:10; 2 Corinthians 5:10; Revelation 20:11–12; Psalm 75:7; Psalm 9:8; Ezekiel 33:20. Which one applies most specifically to Port Royal in 1692 and then to you today?

Unsinkable

Sid Huston

In the suspense of time and space
I'm being lifted by grace
Under God's wing
I am in a good place

Buoyed by love
Lifted by hope
Inspired by faith
Though I get pushed under
By His grace, I rise above

Unsinkable is what I am
Because of His omnipotent hand
Unsinkable is what I am

By your blessings, I stand
Before kings, I stand
Against the tide and the
Spirit of the age, I stand
Because I am unsinkable,
I take a stand

Up straight, I stand
Salvation is the grace to stand
Wisdom and the Spirit
Help me to stand
In glory, I happily stand

Fear sinks into the sand
Knowing I am unsinkable
Like a gourd when I am pushed down
I ascend through the water
In the sunshine, I gleam

He says the word
And the waves and the tide subside
"Peace be still'
Even nature has to abide
I am safe by His side

I am unsinkable
My eyes are fixed on Him
He is so great
He walks on the water

Buoyed by love
Lifted by hope
Inspired by faith
Because of His promise
Because of His presence

Though I get pushed under
I always rise above
I am unsinkable
Again and again
He restores my soul

His goodness and mercy
Causes fear and doubt to flee
What does this truth do to me?
I am unsinkable
He says: "Peace be still."

Trials are often part of His will

They develop character, trust, and verve
To lean in to the pain is just what He did
And I have the nerve not to swerve
I am unsinkable

My eyes are fixed on Him
My "water-walking" friend
My Savior, life without end

"He calmed the storm to a whisper
And stilled the waves"
(Psalm 107:29, NLT).

Say it again,
Sing it loud and clear
I am unsinkable

Deists Take a Dive

The waters in Port Royal's deepwater bay are still murky, and the tides keep dredging up more dead bodies.

Before the earthquake, Earl, with the help of his majestic and trusted steeds, had plucked out of the garden area a number of limestone boulders, flat enough for seating. He has assembled them around a firepit outside Tim and Esther's place, which doubles as a gathering place for their church.

Clay had taken it upon himself with Earl and the horses help to build a fire in the pit, and the group, though exhausted from a difficult day of taking care of the dead, performing respectful burials, and tending to the needs of grieving people, needed to sit around the fire and talk and trust their souls to the One who understands grief: "The God of all comfort." They gathered, knowing that God would meet with them and mend their souls.

Papa wanted his little flock to know God was with them, for them, and paying attention to their needs. He wanted to remind each one of God's personal love and care. Often, he would remind them of the lilies in the field, and the birds in the air, and how God put so much creative energy into these small things. He just wanted each one to know they are in His "much-more" care.

The fire was taking hold, and now this little church is enjoying being together, and they wanted to discuss, how could a good God let this happen?

Just as the embers were popping, so were some of these thoughts, and Papa was aware of the rumblings. As the sun was setting and the fireflies were entertaining, Papa said, "I want you to be careful about the lies that are surfacing."

Chase, with Frieda the perky parrot perched on his shoulder, was prone to add a hearty "Amen" at inappropriate times. Chase asked, "What lies are you hearing about?"

Papa said, "That this mess happened because God isn't here, that He doesn't care, or that He is impotent and couldn't do anything about it."

Frieda popped off, "Amen." Chase said, "Bad bird." Frieda squawked "Bad bird, bad bird."

Chase said, "I know that I have had lots of those thoughts. This devastation *addles* my mind. Maybe it's good to be busy. We know sickness and disease can drape us like a London fog."

Tim chimed, "Easy on old London Town."

Chase continued, "This is a scary time for all of us. Our minds are confused, and many of us look like we have just seen the *kraken*." The group laughed, and they needed to.

Tim followed up with his own thoughts. "Papa, you have taught us that God has numbered every hair on our heads, not a sparrow falls without God's knowledge, and every flower is by his making. So, in my mind, I know He knows what is going on here. I believe He cares, and I believe He is here. But why did He allow this to happen?"

Papa was encouraged that they were talking and said, "It is good for us to lean on each other and to express our faith in God. As you know, some people are using this calamity as an opportunity to doubt. They choose to believe the lie, a terrible lie about God, saying that He is not here, that He is not aware, and He doesn't care." The group was nodding their heads in agreement, and Papa could tell they needed assurance of God's love and care.

Papa continued, "Remember when God met Moses at the burning bush? And Moses was up to the challenge of going before Pharoah; yet, He wanted to know, 'Who do I say sent me?' Reasonable, huh!"

Esther chimed in, "This is where God said His name is 'I Am'."

Papa responded, "Very good, Esther. Moses was to take with him God's identity, and we need to do the same. It is not just to try harder, do more work, and be busy. Jesus is our Immanuel, meaning, *God with us*. We are to practice His presence and do all that we need to do with Him, and by His strength and wisdom, with His abiding help, by the Holy Spirit, our *Comforter*.

"There are people who are deists. These people think God is the Creator, but think and act like He is not involved in everyday affairs on planet earth, like right here and now."

The group was following along intently, nodding their heads and agreeing. Papa continued, "They think God poured Himself into creating this world and everything in it, but was too busy to manage it, or became disinterested and went on and got involved in other things. They think He doesn't care, and He is not a personal God, whom we can know intimately."

Clay, who only knows how to speak rough and gruffly, said, "So, He made all of this and left us to ourselves, argh?"

Papa said, "That is what a deist thinks."

Tim winced and said, "They miss the whole point. God made all of this for us, and He made us for Himself. It has always been about relationship. He made us for Himself and saved us for Himself."

Chase affirmed, then added, "But to see what He made destroyed, plundered, and lopped into the bay. It doesn't make God out to be a loving, caring Father. I can see how a person can be confused about God and think God doesn't care. I believe He does, but it can *addle* the mind!"

Esther said, "Our Abba, Daddy, Father, says we are the 'apple of His eye'."

Tim said, "How about the flowers, the hummingbirds, and the beauty of the earth? I think creation tells us that God is here and that He cares."

Papa responded, “A deist thinks God set all of this earth in motion, even the seasons and the storms and the like.”

Tim interrupted, asking, “So, did God sink Port Royal?”

Papa waited for a moment then said, “You have heard me say, not a hair, not a sparrow, or a flower is unnoticed and uncared for by our Creator and ever-present God. Yes, He was aware of the decadence, depravity, and the sinning in Port Royal.”

Chase rang out, “*Blimey me*, somewhere in the Bible I heard that God is a jealous God and an avenging God.”

Papa said, “Yes, this is true. We like to just think about how loving and kind He is, but He is holy and righteous, and He is full of wrath. And it does say the LORD takes vengeance on His adversaries. Let’s not forget God’s nature and character. He is holy and righteous, and this requires that He judge sin.”

Clay cleared his throat and stated, “*Land ho,* this is why Jesus died, *arrr*!”

Esther, with her quiet spirit, intoned, “But Papa, didn’t God judge all our sin on the cross where Jesus died?”

Papa said, “Yes, He did judge our sin on that cross. We who believe in Him, and we who take Him at His Word. His wrath against us has been appeased. But His nature never changed, and by no means does the

Lord leave the guilty unpunished. He has stayed active, and He had had enough. We read about what He did to Sodom, and we have heard about Pompei."

Clay asked, "What did He do there?"

Tim said, I was taught that they were called 'the wickedest cities in the world,' and now they are no more."

Chase quipped, "*Blimey me*! Paybacks are rough." Frieda pipped, "Amen!" Everyone laughed and chuckled.

Clay was clear, "I can just see the ground opening up and those pirates falling to their judgment in the dark, the dank, and the deep."

Chase opined, "Where they are going is also, loud, dark, and hot. Where there is gnashing of teeth, screaming, and endless suffering."

Tim agreed and said, "*Aye*! God's holiness requires it." A holy hush overcame the group, and they sat quietly.

And then Esther began to sing. She sang about God's grace and mercy, asking God to make her a channel of His peace. She sang, "Where there is hatred, let me sow love. Where there is injury, pardon; where there is doubt, faith; where there is darkness, light; where there is sadness, joy." It was a beautiful and timely song often sung by the Friars, to whom Papa once belonged. The group sat in God's grace and felt embraced by the presence of God.

Papa affirmed the presence of the Lord in their midst and in prayer thanked Him for His grace and mercy. Grace to accept what He was doing, and mercy as they, too, acknowledged that they have not received the punishment they deserved for the sins in their lives. Each one was grateful for God being merciful to them and they expressed themselves in humble prayer.

Papa tried to recite a passage he had heard from the Bible: "The LORD has His way, in the whirlwind and in the storm, and the clouds *are* the dust of His feet. He rebukes the sea" (Nahum 1:3–4, NKJV). He continued, "When the storms of life come, the wicked are whirled away, but the godly have a lasting foundation" (Proverbs 10:25, NLT).

Tim replied, *"Yo, shiver me timbers,* He shook that wicked city, the ground liquified, and fell into the sea."

Papa went on, "And the day has come where the deists have taken a dive and saw Port Royal submerged, and all the world has seen. For now, it all looks muddy and murky. We know no one can stand before His indignation. No one can endure His anger. Remember He broke the rocks into sand and made the city slide into the sea."

Esther reminded everyone, "He saved us by His grace."

Clay stated, "I think some righteous folk perished, too."

Papa nodded his agreement and said, "But now they are with the LORD; the sheep get mixed with the goats, and the wheat is entangled with the tares."

Clay went on, captured by the scene in his mind, "Those drunk with drink got swallowed up, went straight down, gurgling and gasping, and then covered up with sand, their souls sent to hell. That is where they belong; their bodies feed the fish. Their god is the devil."

Papa was dumbfounded and asked, "Clay, where did you get that?"

Clay said, "I have been listening to your Bible teaching."

Tim elbowed Clay, "And here I thought you were only coming to see Julie. I didn't know you were paying attention."

Clay defended himself, "*Gangway*, shoot fire, God has been working on me. I know He is here, and He is alive. I know heaven is real, and so is hell."

The fire continued to flicker. The group is exhausted, full of questions, but full of faith.

Not one to make a scene, Clay stands up and quotes John 3:16, "For God so loved the world that He gave His only begotten Son, that whoever believes in Him should not perish but have everlasting life."

As sweet as a deep-gruff voice can sound, Clay went on, "I can't stomach how gruesome this has been. We all feel keelhauled, but, yet, we had the grace to do what we had to do. *Oh, sink me,* God's love has helped us do this. I can't answer the why question, why did this happen? But I believe, now more than ever. God loves us."

Chase then echoed a hearty "Amen." While gazing at the twinkling stars, everyone could see his radiant smile reflecting from the amber glow of the hot embers. The wood was popping, the fireflies were entertaining, and the group was feeling the love from one another, and Chase expounds. The next verse in that passage says, "For God did not send His Son into the world to condemn the world, but that the world through Him might be saved" (John 3:17, NKJV).

"Me hearties, these questions we have spoken of, might have had me *addled* years ago. But now I know I am saved. The Spirit of God has shown us this. I am happy to say that me *scurvy pirate flesh* didn't prevent me from knowing the assurance of salvation. Think of it, we are saved. By grace we are going to heaven to be with Him." Frieda perked up with a squawk, "Heaven, heaven, heaven. *Arrr.*" An enthusiastic flourish! The group laughed and felt God's embrace, as affirmed by God through the personality of a simple, colorful, and obnoxious bird.

Papa, while looking into the crackling fire, gleamed and expressed his thanksgiving to God.

In their next church service, Papa reflected on the following, "We have happy memories of the godly, but the name of a wicked person rots away" (Proverbs 10:7, NLT).

"The hope of good men is eternal happiness; the hopes of evil men are all in vain. God protects the upright but destroys the wicked. The good shall never lose God's blessings. But the wicked shall lose everything" (Proverbs 10:28–30, TLB).

Chew on This: Do you think there is a rational case for deism? Why or why not? Do you see God as active and personal? Are you intimately involved with Him? If so, how does this show in your life? According to Nahum 1:2–6 (NKJV), God is a jealous God. And it says, "The Lord will take vengeance on His adversaries." Do you think He has the right to do this? If so, why? What does His holiness and righteousness have to do with vengeance?

Sail on Unsinkable

"Therefore, put to death your members which are on the earth: fornication, uncleanness, passion, evil desire, and covetousness, which is idolatry. Because of these things the wrath of God is coming upon the sons of disobedience, in which you yourselves once walked when you lived in them (Colossians 3:5–7, NKJV).

"Therefore, as the elect of God, holy and beloved, put on tender mercies, kindness, humility, meekness, longsuffering, bearing with one another, and forgiving one another, if anyone has a complaint against another; even as Christ forgave you, you also so *must do.* But above all these things put on love, which is the bond of perfection" (Colossians 3:12–13, NKJV).

Living Unsinkable

Everyone in and around the remnant of Port Royal was walking in fear and trepidation. Most of the residents could still feel the tremors and rumbles in their feet and in their human spirit. They all needed their minds to be renewed and their hearts to find rest and peace in God. It really is difficult to witness such a spanking and not want to cover your own rear. In the few days that followed the devastating earthquakes and tsunami, 3,000 more souls perished as a result of their injuries and the rapid spreading of diseases and infections that attacked the area.

In the Bible, we read that God's perfect love casts out fear (1 John 4:18). But that doesn't mean our knees won't knock in fear. The witness of the Spirit of God must begin to comfort these precious souls in Port Royal, or worry will overtake them. We have heard about Judgment Cliff. It is now a 1000-foot face of half a mountain, a sheer drop you don't want to fall off. Judgment Cliff resulted when the mountain was torn in two. Now it has a hard, steep, sheer face, but in the spiritual realm, everyone will have to face judgment cliff. Everyone will give an account for their life and come before the Judge. But there is a way to be confident about it. A way that translates into being unsinkable (Hebrews 9:27; James 5:3; 2 Peter 2:5–9, 3:7,10; 1 John 4:17–18; Jude 1:7,15,23).

Fear was dominating the souls of these survivors. A London type of fog had settled down in this area, like an uncomfortable blanket of thorns. The rumors were being exaggerated and were haunting these precious people. They had seen the remains of the rock-hewn jail house dropped into the sea, and only the door frame remained above ground. Where were the prisoners? Where was the notorious Pirate "Red Legs" Greaves?

Rumor has it, he was imprisoned there to be tried and hung for his crimes while pirating.

"Red Legs" was born to Scottish parents who were enslaved to a pirate ship. Red was born in Barbados. He was orphaned at an early age and sold to a cruel and violent master. But he was able to escape by swimming to his freedom across Carlisle Bay and stowed away on a pirate ship, preparing to leave Barbados.

Thinking he was free, he was disappointed by discovering that he was now under the stern hand of Captain Hawkins. This sea captain was known for being brutal, torturing captives, and doing worse to women. Back in the day, sea captains didn't leave much to chance, as you have heard, "dead men tell no tales." Therefore, he ruled with an iron fist. As you know by now, pirates didn't know how to or care enough to build lasting life-giving relationships. Though Captain Hawkins was despised and feared by his crew, he was respected for the rich prizes he took in raiding as a pirate. Pirates learn that the ends justify the means.

Red probably picked up the name "Red Legs" because he maintained a Scottish tradition and wore a kilt; consequentially, his legs were sunburned red. These Scottish pirates were considered "poor whites," because they were.

Red became a very skilled and capable sailor. However, he deeply resented being forced to serve and had great disdain for Captain Hawkins. Red had all he could humanly take, and he sought revenge against Captain Hawkins. When things came to a head, he did the manly thing and challenged Captain Hawkins to a classic duel. Red prevailed, and he killed the brutal captain. This knowledge about Red had the remaining locals fearing for their lives. Was he lurking around? Was he crazed? The legend of "Red" had legs!

In a short while, Red was elected captain of the ship. He drew up reasonable and humanitarian articles of agreement. The crew respected his leadership, and the direction of the ship was under a new quality of character and command.

The history about Red is scant, but the following is what we have heard. Under Red's leadership, his crew had a record of sailing with honor. And his crew showed respect to him, not because anything was forced on them, but because his leadership resembled the Golden Rule. Though Red was known for honor, he pledged to never raid poor coastal villages. But in a moment of weakness, they did sack Margarita Island (off the coast of Venezuela); even though they didn't harm a soul, they ran away with a vast horde of gold and pearls.

It is the author's guess, that having made plenty of loot, he retired on the island of Nevis to the quiet life of a planter. Unfortunately, one of his victims recognized Red and turned him in to the authorities for the bounty on his head. It is true that the crimes were stacked up against him, requiring the judge in Port Royal to sentence Red to hang in chains.

When the survivors got to the jail, the prisoners were gone and fear caused these traumatized people to tremble with adrenaline coursing through their veins. The story of Red goes: after being bounced by the tsunami into the bay, he came to his senses and swam to a whaling ship. He must have been a great swimmer, as several times he saved his own life by swimming.

He remained unsinkable and lived a long life—40+ extra years—and we do not know where, when, or how he died on the Island of Nevis as a gentleman farmer. He devoted his life to helping the poor. It is the author's idea that he reclaimed or dug up the vast horde of gold and pearls and used the proceeds to care for the poor. Reckoning that the "wealth of the wicked was stored up for the righteous" (Proverbs 13:22), he chose to do good.

Yet, there is another man who lived to tell about the Port Royal earthquake and devastation, too. His name is Lewis Galdy. History records that he was in the rock-hewn jail house in Port Royal. (Perhaps with Red, and wouldn't you love to have listened in to their conversations?) Lewis is a man who was buried twice by the earthquakes. The first time occurred while in the jailhouse. It sunk straight down, and he was buried alive. After the second shock, the tsunami lifted him up out of the pit and spit him up to the shore, only to be buried again in the sea by the backwash. He managed to stay afloat until a boat rescued him. He should have been nicknamed "Jonah."

Years earlier, with his brother Laurent, they left France for their faith. King Louis XIV was forcing Huguenots (Protestants) to convert to Catholicism, as he had declared Protestantism illegal. Therefore, these Christian Huguenots were forced against their will to convert. Because of their conviction about Christian freedom, they chose to flee. These precious people with Christian courage can be traced all around the world. It just so happened that Lewis and Laurent ended up in Port Royal, the "wickedest place in the world." There was not much honorable work for these men, and Lewis resorted to piracy. He got caught and was in prison for his crimes. It is interesting that Port Royal was a pirate haven; yet, getting caught as a pirate was still against the law.

His tombstone reads as follows:

> "Here lies the body of Lewis Galdy, who departed this life at Port Royal on December 22, 1739 aged 80. He was born at Montpelier in France but left his country for his religion and came to settle on this island where he was swallowed up in the Great Earthquake in the year 1692 and by the providence of God was by another shock was thrown into the sea and miraculously saved by swimming until a boat took him up. He lived many years after in great reputation. Beloved by all and much lamented at his death."

On top of this tombstone were the words in French: "*Dieu Sur Tout*," or "God Above All."

Certainly, Lewis believed he could look forward into the future with confidence because he believed in the God of all hope. It was as if God threw him a ring of sealed gourds and saved him. He learned to float joyfully in freedom in the current of God's grace. He practiced thanksgiving, which is the key to everything (Romans 1:21; Philippians 4:4–7).

Faith in God makes us unsinkable. So, we need to become a member of the "living wall" made of irregular stones (1 Peter 2:4–6). This wall will support you in your life. It does your soul good to know that you belong in the fellowship of believers. Join good people like Papa, Esther, Tim, Chase, Nick, Clay, Wendolyn, Earl, Julie, and colorful Frieda and others and support each other when the storms of life come, "but the godly have a lasting foundation" (Proverbs 10:25, NLT).

Know also you are wheat and not a weed (Matthew 13:24–30). Jesus is a friend of sinners, this is true, and we must live with some weeds, noxious and binding as they are. Just know that bad company does corrupt good morals, and you must intentionally work to develop a positive life support group of friends. Do not let wicked pirates sink you down.

As wheat, you become positive and life-giving seed for this world. Jesus said as a grain of wheat must die, and then it will rise again. This is your true identity because you believe in Jesus. Resurrection is your true identity. We died with Jesus, and we, too, are raised with Him and are eternally secure with Him and assured of heaven.

Truly you do not need to fear the impending judgment to come. Because you have heard His Word and you believe in Jesus, therefore, you will not come into that judgment. For you have passed from death into life (John 5:24; Romans 10:17).

As you go on, bloom where He plants you. You do not always get to pick your environment, but "tend the garden." Just remember with time, water, sunshine, and wholehearted devotion, you will grow and God will be glorified. You will bear fruit that lasts and have an abundant life (John 10:10, 15:1–8). You are unsinkable, and you will glorify God.

When your world sinks, and it will, you have grace for that (Ephesians 2:8–10). God really loves you, and Jesus has already paid for all your sins by shedding His blood and dying for you on the cross. You are not a pirate anymore: you are a CROWN- wearing child of the living God. All this is by His grace, and He is committed to save you forevermore, that means like Lewis and Red, and He will keep on saving you. You are unsinkable.

So, go ahead and attempt to do good. Try to help the poor as Red and Lewis did in their golden years. This activity has a return on your investment, and is opposite of the pirate way. Because you are unsinkable, you will live with a wonderful uplifting sense of buoyancy, as you walk in the power of the Holy Spirit. So, live brightly, love deeply, and shine like a star by Basking in the sunshine of God's love.

"Dieu Sur Tout" God above all!

Chew on This: How can hope make a positive difference in your life? What are some of the ways God has saved you? Which one are you most thankful for? How does this motivate you, (encourage) you to do good?

Selected quotes from St. Francis:

"All the darkness in the world cannot extinguish the light of a single candle."

"The only thing ever achieved in life without effort is failure."

"Do few things but do them well. Simple joys are holy."

"I have been all things unholy, if God can work through me, He can work through anyone."

Latin phrase: "*Primo Ounctio et Postea Speculations.*" (Holiness first and then learning)

"While we have time, let us do good." From Stephen Siller of Tunnel to Towers. His parents were Franciscans.

Note: Got to admit that we are *addled* to get the definitive scoop about Red Legs Greaves. The evidence about his life, work, service, and death is scarce. But, lots of hearsay stuff. Don't want to *hornswaggle* ya, but, *shiver me timbers*, nothing about his story is etched in granite.

The Ballad of Lewis and Red

Sid Huston

In this ballad of Lewis and Red
You will soon see these gents had nothing to dread

It was a typical balmy Tuesday morning at 11:42
The month was June the year 1692

Fifteen minutes on June seven
To most it was hell, to a few it was heaven

Lewis was walking on the shore
And Red was locked behind the prison door

After three minutes of tremors around the cay
Port Royal dropped in the bay

The fault lines gave way
The wicked met the Lord this day

For sure they got turned away
For there was hell to pay

But, for Lewis and Red
The water they would tread

Lewis got "baptized" twice
The earthquake was more than a roll of the dice

A tsunami recoiled and took Lewis under
But like a buoy, he came up from asunder

Yet, Port Royal got plundered
A pirate haven, a real "one-hit wonder"

This wasn't a mere blunder
A wicked city that makes the righteous shutter

There were liquefaction and rumbles
Then more than 2,000 structures tumbled

On the 53 acres around the harbor
But, oh, the sinking horror of pirate lore

Some built of wood and others of brick
And they fell deep below with the crack of the whip

Both Lewis and Red were able to swim to a ship
Red to a whaler and Lewis to a fishing rig

I don't know if these two ever met
But the details they wouldn't sweat

As the stories get told
This one of Lewis and Red doesn't get old

For certain it needs to be told
Because people can learn of God's faithful hold

Lewis left France and was a merchant
Dealt in cocoa, wine, slaves, and
became the church warden

He marshalled the building of St. Peter's Church
Because to Him faith hadn't left him in the lurch

After another 47 life-filled and fruitful years
His tombstone didn't jeer

It cheers: "God Above All"
His life showed the providence of God
As for Red, he was being tried for being a pirate
In truth, he had become a pirate hunter

He had a heart for the downtrodden
And went to the island of Nevis and
would be known for his garden

Serving the poor and doing good
A life of service is not just "chopping wood"

Why did God save these two?
For two-thirds of Port Royal died at 11:42

Two thousand more would succumb
to disease and vandals
Was this a divine scandal?

I hope these thoughts are not too hot to handle
But judgment day is going to happen

So, learn your lesson from Lewis and Red,
Lewis Galdy and "Red Legs" Greaves

They demonstrate there is a wide road to destruction
But they were on the narrow road that leads to life

There is another lesson to learn
And only the spiritual can discern

Jesus said something about building a house
First clear the sand, gravel, and debris

For in the end, it is not about what you achieve
But in whom you believe.

Jesus said:
"Whoever comes to Me, and hears my sayings and
does them, I will show you whom he is like:
He is like a man building a house, who dug
deep and laid the foundation on the rock.
And when the flood arose, the stream beat
vehemently against that house, and could not
shake it, for it was founded upon the rock.
But he who heard and did nothing is like a man
who built a house on earth without foundation,
against which the stream beat vehemently;
and immediately it fell. And the ruin of that
house was great" (Luke 6:47–49, NKJV).

Every person has an important date
And do not think that it is just fate

For wisdom and faith
Will give you a life like Lewis and Red

Then you, too
Can live without dread

God's amazing love makes you secure
For His perfect love casts out fear!

About Sid Huston

Sid Huston's background in Christian education and his avid interest in history inspired him to create pirate-themed stories of historical Christian fiction, featuring Christian living. He and his wife, Karen, live in Colorado Springs, Colorado.

www.ingramcontent.com/pod-product-compliance
Lightning Source LLC
LaVergne TN
LVHW010657110826
845149LV00014B/3130